Duchess *of* Nothing

By the same author

Schooling

Duchess *of* Nothing

A Novel

Heather McGowan

BLOOMSBURY

Published by Bloomsbury Publishing, New York and London
Distributed to the trade by Holtzbrinck Publishers

All papers used by Bloomsbury Publishing are natural, recyclable products made from wood grown in well-managed forests. The manufacturing processes conform to the environmental regulations of the country of origin.

Library of Congress Cataloging-in-Publication Data

McGowan, Heather.
Duchess of nothing : a novel / Heather McGowan.
p. cm.
ISBN-13: 978-1-59691-066-9
ISBN-10: 1-59691-066-6
1. Rejection (Psychology)—Fiction. 2. Abandoned children—Fiction.
3. Divorced women—Fiction. 4. Rome (Italy)—Fiction. 5. Boys—
Fiction. I. Title.

PS3563.C36495D83 2006
813'.6—dc22
2005018197

First U.S. Edition 2006

1 3 5 7 9 10 8 6 4 2

Typeset by Westchester Book Group
Printed in the United States of America by Quebecor World Fairfield

Look at your brother, I tell the boy as we hang out over the balcony to watch Edmund walk across the courtyard on his way to the street. The ways of your brother are certainly mysterious, I say, But he provides for us so we must never question them. As you know, your brother provides food, shelter and cigarettes; I provide education and comfort, but you, I say sadly, You are not useful at all. You are seven and seven-year-olds are takers only. In their constant yelping for things brought or poured, their complaints about cold feet as well as the inability to walk with any sort of haste, a seven-year-old is completely useless. At least in today's society, I add. Not so long ago children happily pulled a cart or stitched a rug. Alas we live in a different world now.

Below us Edmund closes the gate to the courtyard, disappearing into the city's yellow haze. The boy and I stand together peacefully watching Edmund's back make its way down the street. Your brother has never been a great thinker, I murmur.

No, no, Edmund is a sparrow. Still, we appreciate the sparrow for what he gives us. We do not ask the sparrow to inveigle us with talk of sunsets. We do not ask the sparrow to possess the mind of a poet or the plumage of a parrot. The sparrow is the one mistaking glass for air. It is the self-bludgeoning aeronautics of the sparrow that has us starting from the dinner table. Because of this, the sparrow lives on; he does not get slaughtered for his pretty feathers or his tasty flesh. Perhaps no one has ever accused Edmund of having a great mind, but he is the one we rush to watch stroll across the Piazza Navona or the Via Veneto. The beauty of your brother's back mitigates certain defects like his brain, I remind the boy.

Wrapped in our sheets, the boy and I like to hang out over the window gate to watch Edmund's serpentine path across the courtyard every morning, save those mornings the brother is too chilled. He is a sensitive child who feels the cold excessively, especially in the mornings, when this foul city feels polar. The courtyard below us is empty now and the boy is stretching out his arms to be lifted because he hates the feeling of bare feet on the tiled corridor. Though he is seven and by all appearances old enough to walk down the blessed corridor by himself, Edmund's brother prefers to be hoisted on my back and borne to the kitchen like a little king, like a junior emperor of some faraway nation chosen to lead while he lay swaddled in the cradle with unfocused eyes. And like an obedient servant, I bear him as he wishes. On most days. On some days I lie in bed and smoke cigarettes and wish I were in a faraway nation myself. But today I let the boy clamber onto my back. Today I weave down the hall to the kitchen where I set the boy in one of the yellow chairs bequeathed to Edmund by his father. Edmund's father gave him the chairs on the condition Edmund also accept the boy. Of course this is not how Edmund puts it; this is how I put it. Edmund has a different version altogether. He would never link the yellow chairs to his brother's presence, but for that account you must turn to Edmund's notes, which number precisely zero. Instead, I am the one left to describe Edmund's father drinking his way up the coast of Spain, madeira by madeira. Edmund will mumble when asked what happened to the second wife; I will be the one doing justice to the thunderstorm, the librarian who accompanied her, their rain-soaked journey north. But before daddy's recent wife set off with her lover and two hundred hardcovers rapidly incurring fines, she left the boy with Edmund's father. And before Edmund's father set off on his drinking holiday, he deposited the boy along with four yellow chairs with Edmund and me in Rome.

There are days, days when Edmund's back seems a little tarnished, that I have cast about our rooms wondering what tantalizing treasure I can offer someone to take the boy off my hands. Today is not that day. Today Edmund's back has pleased me to such a degree that I hum as I set about boiling the boy's milk. I am not above breakfast now and then, a real breakfast I mean, not just a cigarette. A cigarette seems like the breakfast of a driven person with many complicated duties to perform throughout the day and several lists in the making. I am not this person; I have no lists. Yet, while no one has ever called me *driven* as such, there was a time when I did things with a quicker step and lighter heart than I do today. There was a time when I did not live with Edmund or his brother. There was a time when I had a husband, and a time before that when I had neither Edmund nor a husband, but was simply myself. This was the time I spent working in a bank some ways from the village where my husband kept a compound. And while I was not driven, I loved my time at the bank before my husband stole me away. I loved counting crisp notes with finicky precision; I reveled in the authority of pushing the correct number of bills across to a customer. It is quite impossible to say how much I enjoyed it and how distinctive each day felt when in fact every day was nearly identical. In the evenings I would return to my small room, where I would boil a cup of hot water and gaze out of the window. I might add some powdered broth to the water or, when given to extravagance, a peppermint teabag. How I loved to stand by the window stirring lazily as I brought my focus to the street below or to the wild meadow that lay beyond it. I had read books that featured protagonists contemplating views with hot drinks and in my move away from home to that small city I longed for nothing more than novel experiences. So many things seemed to lie outside my windows though in truth there was only a barbershop followed in rapid succession by a series of empty lots. You see, I tell Edmund's brother as I take the saucepan of milk from the stove, What matters in life is the promise things hold. Whether or not that promise ever comes to pass does not matter. By the time we discover the thing we hoped held promise holds no such promise, we have found a new thing in which to believe. My future held a great deal of promise when I worked at the bank, I tell Edmund's brother as I hand him his bowl of milk. You would scarcely believe it to look at me now. I learned a number of transactions and specialty procedures that were only ever taught to clerks of exception. I learned, for example, how to identify counterfeit bills, I say. And, unlike the other girls who were cretins bar none, I extrapolated this skill to circumstances outside of the bank and soon made it my business to recognize fakes of all kinds. Then one spring day my husband walked into the bank in a small felt cap and withdrew me, along with fifty-five bills of our smallest denomination. He brought me to his compound on a distant hill, where he methodically began to drive me mad. My husband was Bavarian and I am not, I tell the boy. I never understood a word he said but I accused him of mumbling rather than face my own shortcomings. I regret that now, I add. From time to time. Certainly I could take some blame for our failure as a couple, but you see I choose not to. In the evenings, I continue, My old husband and I enjoyed sitting across from each other at a small table. We liked to fold our hands and avoid each other's gaze. Marriage is like that, I tell the boy, A regular tomb. I tap the packet of cigarettes against the kitchen table for emphasis.

The table is quite empty save the boy's bowl and my packet of cigarettes and our assorted hands. A real tomb, I repeat, my eyes scanning the table surface abstractedly. Where is your green notebook? I ask suddenly, I don't see it here. The boy shrugs, his eyes go up to the ceiling then come back to rest at a point beyond my shoulder. In the bedroom, he says quietly. In the bedroom, I repeat. Fancy that, in the bedroom. Edmund's brother picks up his bowl of milk, watching me over the rim. Frankly, I'm baffled, I tell him. Have we not begun the day? Do you not think something might arise worth penciling in your green notebook? Edmund's brother nods slowly. Well then I can hardly imagine what purpose your notebook is serving in your bedroom. I cross my arms and lean back in my chair. For a disquieting moment I think I might pitch backward and smash my head on the kitchen floor. The boy flinches, eyes wide with alarm. Quickly I steady myself, leaning forward on my elbows. These chairs, I murmur. Chairs will be the death of me. I pull out a cigarette and point it at the boy. I would like you to have that notebook with you on today's expedition, I say. So mind you bring it. He looks about the kitchen vaguely. Where was I? I ask, turning to the stove to light my cigarette. I will die in the middle of some repetition. Husband, he says. Yes, yes, I say, But at what juncture? Edmund's brother stares up at the ceiling.

Marriage is a tomb, he recites. Aha, I say, Clever boy. Now, my old husband was neither attractive nor stupid but average in all ways, I say. Except perhaps that he suffered a great deal. Yes, that man suffered more than anyone has a right to suffer, though he lives in a nice compound in the hills. The rich suffer too, let's not forget. Let's spread a little charity where we can. As you know, my husband married me in error, believing me to be a sort of woman I am not, I continue. Many men make that mistake upon walking into banks, I tell the boy, They notice a woman in immaculate clothes, remark how happily she complies with requests. They admire a demeanor that seems to guarantee subordination but months later are quite surprised to find their bank teller setting fire to things.

It was all my fault, I admit sadly though I think no such thing. My husband was a haunted man but for that I claim no responsibility. Edmund's brother is hunched over his bowl, slurping up milk like a cat. Are you listening to a word of this? I ask. The boy nods. Well bowl to mouth then, I tell him, Not the other way around, not mouth to bowl if you please, you are not some cat. Of course the reason I left my old husband is another story, I say, A lesson for a different day, perhaps tomorrow. Today I am warning you about beauty, the fatal mistakes made in its name. I point around the room, encompassing our meager lives with my cigarette. See what happens? I ask. The boy nods, tilting his head. Meow, he says sadly, Meow, he repeats. Meow, meow, meow. Drink your milk, I say nicely, There's a good cat.

The brother mews a soft protest but obediently picks up the bowl between his paws. For about three minutes there were only two of us. You and Edmund, the boy says, robotically. Yes, Edmund and me, I agree, For about three blessed minutes. After you met him in the Alps, he says. Yes, I say, Precisely. I left my husband and I found your brother at the Alpine Inn. What terrible thing happened in the Alps, do you recall? I ask. You fell in love with Edmund's back, the boy says. Exactly, I nod, puffing on my cigarette, Well done. Many people would feel discouraged having a back turned to them over and over. They might feel shame or self-pity. Not me. With no face to behold I made it my business to worship his back instead: the valleys of muscle, the flicker of sinew. Let the masses have their churches, their temples, I needed only the back of your brother. You thought his back was beautiful, the boy prompts. Exactly, I say, But you see how in one fatal second you can go from being a couple in love or something like love, to being three people. Because I came along, the boy says. Yes, and in two seconds I became a dogsbody, an unpaid babysitter, a milk boiler. Where I was once my own person now I am simply the slut who boils your milk; that is the sole definition of my life today. Why? Because of beauty. So I will boil your milk every morning until I die spent and shriveled, bones ossified, death passing quite unnoticed. The boy stares at me, no longer a cat. That's all, I say leaning back and exhaling. That's the lesson. Beauty is fatal, the boy says quietly. If not beauty then love, I say carefully. Love is fatal, the boy amends. Both are hell, I say getting up, Avoid both is your lesson for today. I am not certain if I ever loved Edmund or what that sensation might feel like but it seems responsible to discourage the boy from any sentiment that leads to a bad decision. I pull open a kitchen drawer. From under the chopping knife, I bring out the photograph.

The boy has seen it many times. Edmund, at fifteen, jumping to hit a soccer ball with his head. A few lesser teammates stand perplexed at the edge of the frame, not Edmund. Edmund flies across the center of the photograph toward the ball, hair fanning out, one hand reaching toward a blurred tree. Look at that neck, I say. We gaze at Edmund's profile with quiet reverence. As we do in the morning. Continue to be ordinary, I say, God forbid you turn out like this. The boy seems sufficiently warned; I replace the photograph. Finish your milk, now, I tell him, There's a boy. I watch Edmund's brother bend his head to sniff the bowl before picking it up to drink.

Of course I had a cat once, an actual cat, when I lived with my husband. We liked to read together out by the pool, my moggy and I, before it was drained and became a playground for rats. The boy sets down his bowl. Moggy? He says, burping, What's a moggy? I stare at him. What do you mean, *What's a moggy?* He shrugs. I don't know, what is it? What's a *moggy?* I say, astonished. Moggy is cat. How can you possibly not know what moggy means? The boy presses his lips together. He is itching to burp again but won't take the risk. He can't predict the consequences of burping when I am agitated. Indeed he has upset me beyond belief. There are certain principles we accept as self-evident. That a child shall know his moggy is one. Yes, as naturally as he scribbles a circle atop five sticks and names it *Papa*. I draw out a cigarette. My god, I murmur, What sort of life are you leading with this depleted vocabulary? How many times have I said there is no life without describing it? Have I not drummed that into your intelligence a hundred different times? The boy nods, parting his lips slightly, perhaps risking a silent burp. You will need to write this down, I say briskly. It will not serve you, this treatment of English. A sort of tsking noise has begun in my head and my new cigarette needs lighting. Where are the matches? I ask. Why am I forced to light my cigarette from the stove over and over like some sort of savage? Edmund's brother gets up and disappears into the front room. I will not continue to light my cigarettes in this manner, I mutter, kicking at the chair. I mean, really. The boy returns with a box of matches and expends three or four attempting to light my cigarette. There is nothing he likes better than lighting matches. Enough, I say finally, snatching the box from him, Any more sulfur and I'll sneeze. I light my cigarette and suck on it, staring at the end in disappointment. The boy picks up his bowl again. Of course I was never allowed a pet as a girl, I murmur, Perhaps this is the reason I have always loved the word moggy. I had to wait until I was married to own anything. I tip back in my chair and listen to the boy slurp his milk; I have not thought of my cat in a long time. What a fine cat she was, mouse warrior, though she had nothing to say about the rats in the pool. Nothing would entice my cat to take care of those rats, some of which were as long in body as she was. The cat appeared one afternoon not long after the baffling rite that signaled my nuptials. I had recently left my situation at the bank in order to join my husband and I liked to take my little trowel outside to dig at the mounds of earth, hopeful for gardens of some sort, a blanket of azaleas perhaps or a bed of daffodils. I might have been humming the day my moggy appeared, I might have been that content; it was early days in that slow asphyxiation we know as marriage. As I happily scraped the earth, my skirt was spread about me like a parachute. Unfortunately it was not a parachute and instead of pulling a rip cord I doomed my husband to my unpredictable temper for several years. The sun was pleasantly warm that day; I was enjoying myself immensely when it came to my attention that I was being watched; I turned and found myself forehead to forehead with a dear moggy. And though the cat was well fed, had no fleas and took an instant dislike to me, the idea of rescuing a stray was so overpowering that I scooped up the cat and brought it indoors. From then on the cat rarely left my side. And whether that was due to the string I attached to its collar or to tender feelings on the cat's part, who is to say. I fed and cared for that pepper-spotted cat as if it were my own husband—whom I actually treated rather badly. How many days I would sit and stroke

moggy sweetly under the blistering sun. And when her fur became clammy, when clutches escaped, drifting to settle in my
tea, or lodge in my mouth or nostrils, I never swore or struck
my sweet moggy or threw her in the swimming pool. How patient I was with my cat's cattish travails, listening in earnest to
her sorrowful cries, giving them my ear as I racked my brain for
the most profound interpretations. Across the table Edmund's
brother wobbles his neck kittenishly. Meow, he whispers. But
she never loved me. In fact, she had a certain way of eyeballing
me then attending to an ablution exactly when I most needed
comfort. And in my anguish, how often she would turn to expose the puckered O beneath her tail. Small deaths but deaths
all the same. The boy begins licking his hand. Come on, I say
standing, You are an inauthentic cat and I am tired of cats.

I carry the boy down to his room and we climb into his
bed, arranging the blankets comfortably around our necks. Side
by side we stare at the ceiling for a few minutes in silence. We
call this meditation, I say, In answer to how we begin our day.
This morning we will think about pleasant things for exactly
forty-five minutes, I tell the boy, We will breathe through our
nostrils while recalling situations that give us pleasure. After
that, you may read to me if you wish, then we will go on with
our day's work. Now, what do you plan to think about? I ask
him as a real teacher would, a teacher with a wage packet I
mean. He considers for a minute. I will think about my dog, he
says. Fine, I say, You may think about *a* dog but it is impossible

to think about *your* dog because you have no dog. And as long as I have any say in the matter you will never have a dog. Dogs are machines for smelling and barking and have few redeeming qualities like their cousin the cat. But, he stammers, But I like dogs. A crack in the paint is making its way daily across the ceiling. I have always liked ceilings and found peace there. The more cracked the better. Certainly we have read that the dog will serve us, I say finally. Apparently the dog will tow us from the river when we fall into its icy depths, but such circumstance is rare enough to make the caring for a dog a clear refutation of logic. The boy sighs. I allow Edmund's brother to take his dog for a walk, to open the disgusting tin of dog food and shake it all over the place and pick up his doggy feces and throw and run with his dog as long as I don't have to see it or hear about it. I have things to digest that have nothing to do with animals. I am thinking about predestination, I tell the boy, who makes petting motions to his invisible dog on the ceiling. I am thinking about fate. Lying here next to you, I plan to consider what sort of choices we have in life versus what is simply dished out from up above. I plan to wonder how the hell I ended up here. The boy scratches his head. For example, I say, I could have had a very different sort of life, one that never involved you or your brother. Do you know what sort of person I was before I became your milk boiler? I ask. You had a cat? he says. Yes, yes, but before that. The boy thinks. You had a bank? I did not *have* a bank, I say, People do not *have* banks, as they *have* cars or *have* a disease; they *work* at banks. But you are quite correct, before I was married with a cat I worked at a bank and before I worked at the bank I lived with . . . ? I look at the boy questioningly. He looks pained. I try again, Before I left home, I lived with . . . ? A dog? he says hopefully. Oh for God's sake, I say, I worry for your memory, I really do. Before the bank I was a little girl who lived with parents, I say patiently, And though these parents tried to squeeze their daughter into a little mold, though they forced on her books chosen to ensure she remain obedient and compliant and eighty percent inane, that little girl fought back with her little teeth and nails. Yes, she did, I nod. You see at that time I possessed what they call *potential.* Unfortunately, as my biography will show, this *potential* was robbed by various individuals. Robbed or . . . flayed. In any case, destroyed. By the time your brother Edmund arrived there was barely any potential left for him, but what there was he grabbed, make no mistake. I don't go to school, the boy says, scratching at his head. Once I did, he says, When I lived with my mum and dad. Yes, I say, And while that information is certainly correct it is not relevant. Conversation is the exchange of *relevant* subject matter, not random thoughts flung all over the place, I tell the boy. I was not speaking of school, I was speaking of *potential.* Can you spot the difference? The boy nods, biting his lip. In any event, without allegory, your stories are simply a means of passing time. And nothing bores me more than passing time. Nothing makes me feel my impending death more than the attempt to pass time. The boy looks confused. But I did go to a school, he says, When I was little. I take his hand. How do your fingers get so filthy from eating breakfast? He shrugs and places his hand carefully in his armpit as if to erase it from my memory. School? I say, I have nothing to say about school. When I was a girl I attended a prison of chalkboards. I roamed those halls filled with death, I watched old people robbing the brains of children. Did I learn anything at school? I did not. Unless you wish to include learning not to learn in which case I learned a great deal. Apart from one thing all that schooling added up to a big fat zero. Do you know what that one thing was? I ask the boy. Edmund's brother has closed his eyes. His folded hands rest on his chest. He is playing dead. The game has been off limits since the day Edmund walked in on the boy and me lying dead in the kitchen. A leak from the oven had stolen our lives while we ate lunch. Blankness descended on us in a great snowy sheet; maggots chewed our corpses and our organs distended and turned a rich purple. Squinting through a dead eye, I noticed a spoon in the boy's unconscious hand drooped with a thrilling realism. Oh yes, he shines at the details, this one. I nudge him. Do you know what that one thing was? I ask again. The history prize, the boy intones without opening his eyes. Exactly, the history prize and I'll thank you not to treat it like some passing nothing. The history prize! Edmund's brother exclaims, snapping his eyes open in a mockery of enthusiasm. That's right, I say smugly, Who won the history prize when she was only twelve? You did, the boy says. Exactly. When I was twelve, a whole wild life lay before me. We stare at the ceiling the boy and I because we are living our lives at this very instant, just living them, like single-celled creatures in fluid. The entire town filled the school hall to watch me walk up on stage, shake my teacher's hand and recite my speech into the microphone. Afterward all the mothers and fathers collected in circles to drink execrable wine from plastic cups. Their fat-witted children dismayed them; they spoke of a dog found belly-up in a neighbor's lake. I remember it all quite clearly. My aunt taking me aside to say, You have been rewarded for excelling, but now you must live up to your potential. My aunt was a very wise woman, I tell the boy, You have no idea how intelligent my father's sister was at that time. Before she died, Edmund's brother says. Yes, I confirm, Before she died. My aunt was a woman without compromise. She might have been the only one who did not expect me to end up as a little boy's milk-boiler. Silence. My aunt never had any children of her own, I say. Being childless allowed her to become a person in her own right. Before she died my aunt took many trips to foreign places and brought me back mementoes of her journey every time. I still have them, I tell the boy, Somewhere. Shells mostly for she loved nothing more than to walk beside the ocean. I often suspected my aunt was not my aunt at all, but perhaps my uncle, for she wore trousers and cut her hair extremely short. She was not afraid of anything, I tell the boy. Except children, perhaps. I cannot recall her speaking to me until I was ten. Before that she often took the long way around the room. The boy scratches his head. When I was awarded the history prize, on that day when the entire school came to applaud my intelligence, my aunt clapped the loudest. It was my aunt who led the standing ovation, such as it was. Perhaps it could not be named an ovation exactly since only six or seven followed her lead. But the precise number of people who got to their feet does not matter. After all, the town was noted for its indolence, no one stood if they deemed no emergency or food was to be found at the end of the effort. The boy scratches at his head again. My aunt, with her short hair and traveling ways, had returned to see me accept my award, I tell the boy, And the sight of my father's sister on her feet smashing her hands together loudly is a memory I treasure to this day. Again he scratches. What on earth are you doing? I ask, Why do you keep scratching like that? I leap up, shielding myself with a pillow. You can't just madly scratch like that, I say, If you have head lice they will leap across the bed and take root in my hair. The boy stops scratching; a look of concern crosses his face. We can always shave your head, I say, But mine is another thing entirely. I have long gorgeous hair that gets comments wherever I go and I won't shave it off like some fugitive because you're too lazy to wash your hair. Edmund's brother looks like he doesn't know which way to run. Hold on, I instruct, throwing down the pillow. I race into the living room, returning with a magnifying glass we used during yesterday's physics lesson in which we learned about burning small holes in the living room carpet. Holding the glass up to my eye I inspect the boy's follicles. There is no need to scrimp on hygiene, I tell him, Simply because we are intelligent. From what you see on the streets and in cafés, you might conclude there is some equation between intelligence and body odor but this is not a law by any means. We can read books and shampoo our heads and even find time to wash discreet pockets that require extra care. The boy's head is engrossing in its magnification. You've got a forest here, Mate, I tell him in a friendly Australian way though in fact I cannot speak like an Australian except to use the word mate. I throw down the magnifying glass. No lice? The boy asks, disappointed. Nothing there. He picks up the magnifying glass and aims it at the back of his hand in the hopes of catching a louse on the run. Right, I say, Time to dress. I leave the boy to puzzle out the arms and legs of his clothing and return to the room I share with Edmund. The room is musky but not from love. I smooth the bed covers, pull back the curtains, fold a few of Edmund's shirts and place them in their drawers. Then I snatch my poppy dress, pull it over my head, arrange my hair, arrange it again and whistle for the child.

No bank teller sought truth the way I did, I tell the boy as we make our way across the piazza to Toby's café. Do you think Samina ever boiled a cup of broth and stood by a window? I ask, though I suspect that Samina was never her name. I suspect that the girl who worked next to me at the bank was born with a name no more exotic than Fran, but Samina is the tag she wore on her chest and it is Samina I will call her here. I doubt an original idea ever entered Samina's fat head, I tell the boy, though in fact Samina had a very small head. I don't mean an incisive head, the type dense in its abbreviation; no, Samina's head, though small and pointed, seemed fleshy and obtuse. I will always recall Samina with an enormous fleshy head, though photographs of her could prove otherwise. Photographs of Samina might show the head of a genius, I have no way of knowing. And though I am loathe to cast judgment on my compatriots at the bank, I did so all the time with a great deal of enjoyment and continue to do so now though I am uncertain whether they are living or deceased.

After milk and meditation we always walk to Toby's café for breakfast. Edmund's brother and I hate the café where Toby works, we find it middling, a real haven for the middlebrow, but Toby gives us free pastries and coffee so you will find us there on most days. One morning the boy grumpily pronounced it a café fit for a train station. We found this so hilarious at the time that we insist on repeating *train station café* almost every morning in the hopes of regaining the joke's initial hilarity. We have been to so many cafés the world over, I tell the boy as we take our favorite seat behind some large plants, We can safely assume that ours are palates of the highest order. I like to comfort the boy and include him in my world though in truth I am around only for his brother's back. Edmund and Edmund only is the source of my pleasure. You may think I am a fool for the back of your brother, I tell the boy, But I can walk away in an instant. I have a reverence for it, yes, but this is what we do, we find our things to revere and we revere them quietly. We do not accept instructions of reverence from others, I tell Edmund's brother. Nor do we crow like the declarers of pleasure we pass on the city streets, absolutely not. We unearth small delights and keep them firmly pressed to our chests. This is what I am here to teach, I remind him. When I was seven, I was not like you, lolling around while my hydrocephalic head is filled with ideas. I lived on edge, waiting for a whack, jumping at the smallest sound, forced to read books guaranteed to send me into pits of despair and deny me a freethinking mind. A book about Sally and her insufferable pony, tales of good girls doing good things. God, the horror of that time. I stole adventure tales to read under the blankets, but it was soon enough that I threw them all away, I tell Edmund's brother. As soon as I knew that I could never steer a motorcycle across the country, sleep under the stars or mingle with barroom regulars. Why would I read about adventures in which I could never partake? You will be able to do these things, I say, If you survive your adolescence. Where I am in danger of constant assault, you will be free to roam wherever you like. I will never sleep alone in an open field or walk home at night without fear, I tell him. So you see, where I have failed you must succeed. I will not have you grow into a replica of me. It would be very painful to me if you became my replica and were forced to take your learning where you could, seizing on it like a stray dog instead of sitting at a desk. One day you will have a charming desk and sit in a bright room filled with books and globes, I tell the boy. One day you will have a teacher, you will have the maps they point sticks at, but not today. Not today and not in this fetid city where I have seen teachers flirting and smoking in the playground all too often. I may have been denied what you call a *proper* education, I tell the boy, I may whimper for handouts my whole damn life, but I can still teach you a thing or two. Edmund's brother nods. You may sneer, I say, No doubt you think you already know more than I. What you do not know is that sneering and condescension are traits favored by youth. You will come to know, as I have come to know, that we do not in fact know all we think we know when we are young. A condition of growing older is finding you know less than you thought you knew. I know now that I am in fact far less intelligent than I believed myself to be when I was a child or young adult. And I imagine when I am on my deathbed my final astonishing epiphany will be that I am utterly ignorant of everything. Edmund's brother nods. Have faith in ignorance. Make humility your religion. I like the sound of this and repeat the phrase to myself several times quietly, unsure as to whether I am myself in any way humble but knowing that for the sake of peace, I must demand it of the brother. The boy nods and thrashes his hand under the table, groping his testicles I imagine. I direct his attention to three boys hunched over their books on the other side of the café. You see how you must stuff knowledge in your head like sausage in a casing? I ask. Look at those students, look at that exquisite agony. Learning is the most painful thing to which we apply ourselves, I say, Though marriage is right up there. Marriage is a tomb, the boy says softly. That's right, I say, And we commit ourselves to these painful things. Yes we do. I open my mouth to comment further but Toby has appeared next to us in a frenzy of movement, simultaneously wiping his hands on his apron, flustering at the table with a little rag, and repositioning a chair with his foot. Hello, Toby, I say sweetly, How are you today? Toby shakes his head. How am I today? He repeats incredulously, I'm about up to here. He slashes at his neck with one finger. I have got to talk to Edmund about this, he says, spinning on his heel and rushing away again. What on earth was that about? I say, lighting a cigarette. He has to talk to Edmund about *what* may I ask? The boy stares behind me at Toby's retreating back. It's not like we want to come here, he says, Who wants to come to some *train station café*? Exactly, I agree. Toby acts like it's some sort of honor for us to take breakfast at this horrible place. If he's going to indulge that foul temper while he's at work, I guarantee his manager will have something to say about it. I squint through the smoke of my cigarette. All that action made me feel quite sick, I say. I can't think it's advisable to move so quickly at this hour. The boy shudders in agreement. I wish I could provide you with an adequate role model instead of a drunk like Toby, I add, But there is the free food to consider. Edmund's brother widens his eyes at me and I turn around in time to see Toby approach holding two coffees and a plate of braided pastries. The boy and I smile nicely but Toby dashes away without a word. He knows I hate these pastries, I tell the boy, lifting one. These are the worst pastries in all of Rome. We split five pastries between us, the boy and I, demolishing them ravenously. Then we sit together quietly. I pick sugar from my elbow and Edmund's brother delicately licks his cup clean.

Across the café Toby stands at the coffee machine gazing into a silver jug. His lips move, to some terrifying soliloquy, I imagine. Behind him well-dressed citizens sip their coffees, quietly content being Italian. If you could understand the strength it takes to sit here quietly, I tell the boy, If I had the power to describe how it feels to do exactly the opposite of what I'd like. I wish you could see the storm that rages beneath my surface. I was never meant to sit quietly, I tell the boy, This sitting quietly was never my idea. I flick my skirt idly, exposing my knee. It stares up at me, a hilly rebuke. I want to leave everything behind as soon as it is a minute past new. Every night after supper I'd like to drop the plate I'm washing, turn, never see any of it again. And yet I remain. I swallow my coffee, I remain.

Edmund's brother leans forward across the table. Toby stinks, the boy whispers, canting his head toward Toby, now in retreat, balancing a number of cakes. Really? I ask, sniffing the air. Yes, the boy says, looking pained. He smells like he never takes a bath. Well, I smell nothing, I say. Well, perhaps it has dissipated, the boy answers boldly. Dissipated? Rich words from someone who did not know his *moggy* fifteen minutes prior. I take out a new cigarette and tap it against its packet. I hope you are not becoming arrogant, I tell Edmund's brother, pointing the cigarette at him. The boy gives me a sharp kick under the table. What! I bark, astonished, What the hell was that? The boy motions to Toby walking past and quickly, perhaps before he has even quite passed us, I sniff the air frantically. Hm. I sit back in my seat. Hm. The boy waits to hear my news. *Wellll*, I say judiciously as I light my cigarette and give it a healthy suck, I see what you mean. Edmund's brother folds his arms and smiles, as if I have forgotten that nasty little kick. I don't enjoy maligning others, I say, On the other hand, it is vital to exercise our critical gifts. Imagine if we could not understand Melville the next time we pick him up, I say, That would be a disaster. Critically, Edmund's brother and I watch Toby swerving through the café in his tight trousers. Edmund's brother pinches his nose and sticks out his tongue. Smelly, smelly, he says. There are several things I might add to that assessment, I say, smoothing my belly. The man's clothing clings, for one. Most egregiously, he states the obvious with the measured authority of a half-wit. The boy releases his nose and coughs. Toby is standing directly next to me, bending to place two cups of fresh coffee on frilly paper mats before us. Tell Edmund, he says, collecting our empty cups, You can tell Edmund that I took care of you again this morning. I hand Toby a dirty spoon he has overlooked. Fine, I say with a nice smile. Toby snatches the spoon and storms away. My lord, I say, He really has an odor to him. You don't think it's smoking that makes Toby stink like that, do you? I ask. In the excitment my cigarette has gone out but I am suddenly reluctant to commit to it. The boy takes a sip of coffee then bites the cup. No, you don't smell like Toby, he says. Though I can hear the boy quite well I ask him to repeat himself. I like reiteration. And please don't bite that cup while you're speaking, I add, It impedes your speech. If you want to carry those manners out into the world with you, I'd trouble you not to mention I was once your guardian. I relight the cigarette. Of course, I don't smoke as much as Toby, I say thoughtfully. Toby smokes like a maniac; there are not enough hours in the day for Toby to get all his smoking in. The man must rise in the middle of the night to snatch a few more cigarettes. We watch Toby arranging pastries on a plate in a sort of dumping fashion. I have never been a smoking *maniac,* I remind the boy, A cigarette now and then for digestion's sake, but no one could call me a smoking machine. It has never been my so-called vocation to smoke a million cigarettes. I pick up the new coffee and take two large swallows. Good god but it is hot. The scathing liquid courses into my stomach; I press my fingertips into my brow bone willing away the pain as I used to watch my father do every Sunday evening. Are you alright? Edmund's brother whispers. I nod. You best blow on that before drinking, I say hoarsely, pointing to his coffee. The boy nods. He is a good boy and often does what he is told. When the boy listens and makes notations in the green notebook I bought for that purpose, he is one of the very best seven-year-olds in existence. I challenge you to find a seven-year-old anywhere in the city as bright or charming; though, on other days, half as obstinate and willful. In conclusion, I say, I think we both agree that *excess* smoking is the reason for Toby's odor. That and not bathing. I reach for the coffee cup, staring respectfully at the brown liquid it holds. My body excels at a quick recovery. The misfortunes it receives are usually forgotten only moments later. Edmund's brother blows on his coffee, picks up the cup and takes a cautious sip. I do the same. We both take another. Then another. My heart begins to pound in my chest, something it does rarely. While it is a comfort to know the old boot operates, still an alarm bell rings somewhere. Cases of turbulence in vital organs are a family legacy. By legacy I mean cause of death. On the other hand, the boy is saying, Toby has blue eyes. Yes, we all know that, I answer, though I seldom bother with anyone's eyes. And what do you mean, *on the other hand*? Is there something redemptive about blue eyes? I ask. Does that make the man smell any better? My teeth are clicking; the words won't come fast enough. There's a rabbit in my chest and I have no time for anything. Blue eyes mean less than nothing, I snap.

There are repulsive men and women staring out at the world with blue eyes, men and women so ugly it freezes the blood to come upon them, not to mention the Germans, who, as you know, are a sore spot with me. I am speaking so quickly I am uncertain if it is still English I am using. If you have something intelligent to add to the conversation, I continue, I welcome your thoughts, but if you insist on reeling off inanities in the hope I won't notice, take it elsewhere. I won't listen, I tell him, Perhaps Toby will listen, perhaps Toby will laugh and clap his withered fingers like an organ grinder's monkey, but not me. Not I. Not me. I slam my cup down on the table to indicate that the subject has reached its completion. My command of grammar is slipping. Edmund's brother raises his head from the coffee cup. His eyes swivel around the room, his tongue unfurls and he begins to pant like a dog. I should have read a child-rearing book at some point. I should have found one in a library and checked the glossary under *Coffee*. Across the café, at the students' table, Toby distributes pastries with silver tongs. Tongs! I say to the boy. Do you see that? We never had tongs, we were simply handed pastries; if anything they were thrown at us. And to students! I add as I try to make out if Toby is now bowing to a table of three women or simply stooping to retrieve a fork. I wonder if these women who flirt with Toby know about his vile habits, I say, Though that could be the draw. I've heard of those types. Types that enjoy fetishes. A fetish is an unusual passion that repels others. These women, I point around the café, May have a *fetish* for Toby's rancid odor. Can you use *fetish* in a sentence? I ask, trying to steer the day back to education. Rancid? The boy says, scornfully, That's not a word, *rancid?* I laugh. Of course it's a word, Rancid. Well, I've never heard of it, he says. I pause. I don't like to be tested. Knowledge immediately vacates my head if it senses a test. I'll forget my own name if someone catches me off guard or asks too loudly. Edmund's brother has me in a bind, I suddenly can't recall what rancid means; it might be a city I once visited, if it is even a word at all. Of course it's a word, I repeat. It's a word that means foul, or fetid. Rancid. We repeat it several times, *rancid, rancid,* testing the word in the crowded café, rolling it over on our tongues, my large pinkish one, the boy's small one, thick with coffee, as if this morning it is our job to test words. What a rancid café this is! The boy cries. Rancid as fish on Sunday, I mutter, and what with the coffee and our sudden superiority we both become somewhat hysterical. Oh we laugh and laugh, the brother and I, we have our joy, we do, what with the coffee and all. Then my teeth begin to hurt, they tingle like mad and several patrons are staring. For some reason Edmund's brother has taken to gripping the seat of his chair with both hands and is hopping with it held firmly against his bottom. He stops when I snap my fingers and dart my eyes and together we rush toward the entrance as the boy cries *beep beep.*

Outside, the streets are dense with shoppers swarming to their own logic. What on earth was that dance about in there? I ask, snatching Edmund's brother into a doorway before he is swept down the street. We are panting and addled; I have received a poke from a man's umbrella; there is a pulsing in my veins. But my heart seems calmer. And my teeth feel normal again. The boy pushes at the curb with his toe, I need the toilet, he says, finally. I put a hand on his shoulder. There are words for these delicate functions, you know. He shrugs, jiggling his leg. Dances are for primitives who have no language, I say, leading him across the street toward a large department store. Dances are not for the café where we take our coffee every morning. Come on, I say, above the honking, We shall find you a toilet in the Bisolatti.

From the day I first came to Rome I have hated few things with the intensity I reserve for the Bisolatti. I hate the imperious shadow it casts over the entire street, the way tender saplings shiver outside its entrance. I push Edmund's brother toward the lavatory on the far side of the ground floor. Don't dawdle, I mutter, We have a day's education ahead of us and this place fills me with anxiety. The boy disappears between two racks of men's trousers; I turn my attention to the wares.

Forty varieties of leather gloves lie preserved in vitrines. Behind my back I cup one hand in the other and stare into the cases, examining the exotic species with the learned air of a glove inspector. A woman next to me turns from her own studies. A vulgar hat, a sort of clamshell, sits on her head at a rakish

angle. She looks at me: up from my shoes; down from my décolletage, then turns away with a sniff. My aunt would have eaten
this glove buyer for breakfast. And she didn't need the cheap
pearls to do it. This woman's pearls are strung so tightly I fear
she could choke if she reaches up in haste. Wedges of skin glint
between the tiny globes. If the globes begin to tighten, she
should not count on me for resuscitation. Alas for her, the news
on how many breaths in the mouth and pumps on the chest va-
cated my head long ago. There was a time when I resembled
this woman, though my teeth are my own. There was a time
when I had fresh dresses and considered manners. But I had
the same ugly yellow soul then as I have today. I turn my attention back to the gloves in their glass case. I begin to bend my
head slowly toward the case, lowering it closer and closer as if I
am very near sighted. When my nose reaches the glass, I look at
the woman out of the corner of my eye. She is regarding me
nervously. At this moment, Edmund's brother walks up with a
contented smile and unzipped trousers. Quickly I stand upright, grin at the glove buyer, snatch the boy's hand and pull
him out into the street.

We walk in silence for some time, crossing Via Sallustiana and heading north; or the direction I take to be north. The
alarming sensation produced by so much coffee has lessened.
At the end of the street something will remind me why I came
this way. I cannot get the woman with her pearl necklace out of
my mind. Sniffing as if I had a stink to me. Perhaps not a literal

stink but a figurative one certainly. Was I insulted back there? I ask the boy, Because I feel insulted. I feel very insulted as a matter of fact. I can tell you this about economics, I continue, Revolution may be unseemly to those of us who once worked in banks but sometimes there is a sensible reason to overthrow a government. Look around you, ask yourself how society functions with its suppression of the have-nots. We have come to the end of Via Sallustiana. Edmund's brother looks from side to side. Where are we going? he asks. I light a cigarette and regard the sky. Then I inspect the end of my cigarette as if the boy has asked a particularly provocative question, one that requires deep thought. In fact the question has irritated me beyond measure. Where is your green notebook? I ask quietly, looking past him down the street. The boy shrugs and kicks at something invisible. My god, I say, I don't know why I bother, I really don't. The boy hooks his thumbs into the waistband of his trousers as he does when he feels uneasy. What have you done with it? I ask sensibly. Have you lost it, hm? Do you even know where it is? He pulls at his trousers. It's in my bedroom, he says. I suck on my cigarette. In your bedroom, is it? I repeat, Well, I really think you might bring it with you when we have clearly set out to learn a thing or two. I really think you might. He coughs. Sorry, he says. I take a deep breath. You know, I don't like the turn this day is taking, I tell him, It began very well, we did what we like to do in the morning, we watched Edmund make his way across the Piazza Navona and though I barely slept last night, I would say I listened to your cat noises quite reasonably at breakfast. The boy nods his assent. After that, I continue, puffing on the cigarette, We consumed pastries and though they were not my favorite, in fact though the pastries brought by Toby were my least favorite in all of Rome, you heard no complaint from me. My eyebrows lift; again the brother nods. Added to all this was an idea I had to take you to the zoo. The zoo! he cries. Yes, I say sorrowfully, This morning I had an idea you might like that. Edmund's brother stares at me as if he suspects a trick. Really? he asks. I nod. It came to me as I lay in bed this morning waiting for sunrise that the boy has never seen a tiger or an antelope. That is, to my knowledge he has never seen a tiger or an antelope; there is a distinct possibility that before we met Edmund's brother saw many of these things. It is possible that as a child he lived in India where his father had to shoot the things away from the breakfast table. I never question the boy about his past in case it makes him cry. And while his prior life may include tigers and exotic creatures, my guess is that it does not. My guess, formulated as I lay in bed listening to Edmund's breath come at its steadily irregular intervals, is that the boy's life thus far has been devoid of animals. I would not like to risk the boy developing into someone who cannot tell a goat from a mule. Now I have no idea what sort of zoo Rome has, or if it even has a zoo and while I might have asked Edmund, I have never liked the sound of his voice. Your knowledge of the animal kingdom is suffering in this city, I tell the boy. A child of seven or eight should know the difference between the toads and the seals and the herrings of the world. The boy nods eagerly. I stub out my cigarette. There are mammals and invertebrates and species now extinct that we only find in rocks, I say, There are the things that drop on us and the things we step on. And you will quickly find they all obey strict rules as to body temperature and food preference. Can we see giraffes? the brother asks, eyes bright as that squirrel's and none the less terrifying. There are few animals I loathe more than the squirrel with his insistent eye and bizarre way of sitting up. Yes, I say, turning away, If the zoo carries giraffes, we will visit them. At the zoo we will meet many animals, I continue as we turn and walk back down the street. We will marvel in their differences; we will discover who they befriend and who they eat. Finding the zoo will be our first adventure, I say. First we must find it, then we will go to it. Come on. I tow him across the city by the hand, panting next to me. We walk across several piazzas, turning in the middle of one after the other, unsure if we have been in this particular piazza before. We cross the Tiber, then cross over it again silently, looking for our zoo. For a long time we walk in silence. Finally I speak. It is not to be doubted that the glove buyer makes us feel terrible because that is the function of the glove buyer, I say. Without her, how would we recall how odious we are, how useless and contemptible?

How delicious it is to have our deepest fears of self-hatred utterly confirmed by this woman in her terrible hat, I tell the boy, How comforting to be so miserable. Wear your misery like an inky cloak, I suggest, Let it provide safe harbor from the turmoil of everyday joy. We make our way up a steep street, the nerves in my brain thrumming like piano wire as I struggle to untangle the mixed images of coats and storms. When Edmund comes home tonight worn out from his day's travails, we will lighten his day with our stories of the animal kingdom and how many different things we have learned about life on our planet, I say, The sort of information we require if we are to become whole, entire and empathetic human beings, the type of information kept from us by that strata of society that likes to keep us trapped firmly under its shiny boot, I say, panting slightly, Namely, certain women who like to buy gloves in oppressive shops.

We have reached the top of the street. Below us lies the city, silver and grey, red roofed. All I can make out is the long snake of the Appia Nuova. I need to think a minute, I tell Edmund's brother, I need to remember where I have last seen the zoo. We sit down on a small patch of grass, exhausted by our search. I'm certain I have seen one, I murmur, Somewhere. Near Popolo perhaps. In its glinting way, the light is familiar, so like the glory of those afternoons when I worked at the bank, back before I met my husband, when I was semi-driven. I take out a cigarette and stretch my legs. Next to me the boy collapses on the grass to gaze up at the sky. Were this some other day, some morning I had not borne such great agitation in so few hours, I might have warned Edmund's brother against spoiling his clothes in the dirt. Certainly an ordinary day would not find me lounging on the grass in my one good dress. I may not own a string of pearls but I still have manners; I still enjoy a sense of propriety, at least outwardly.

This light reminds me of the evenings when I worked at the bank, I tell the boy, Before I ever met my husband or your brother. What joy I felt every evening on my way home, swinging my leather case which I had purchased for my first day at the bank and which I carried every day though it remained empty. I enjoyed the case merely for the smell of leather that wafted up to me as I walked, I say. Soon I would regret expenditures that did not function as they were designed to function. But at that time, the time when I worked in the bank, an object that smelled fine remained practical; it did not matter that its purpose differed from the purchased one. In fact when I think of the word *happy* or when the word *happy* is said aloud for whatever reason, even when I read the word *happy* in print, it is always accompanied by the smell of leather. I was ignorant then of how time operates, inching us onward as if by a geared mechanism with no say on our part to its forward movement. It did not bother me then as it bothers me today that I could not step out of time's progress for a day or two to catch my breath and smoke a cigarette. My door opened again and again onto evenings, each one spent quite the same as the one before, an enjoyment of similar food groups, soups or boiled things; things simple to boil, fruit that needed little preparation, from time to time a vegetable if I found the courage to prepare it. I think I am unable, yes I am quite unable to describe the joy those quiet evenings with my small feasts and books brought me. In retrospect perhaps I remember it as joy when it was only habit. It was full of habit, my life then. Oh but retrospect can be so venal; what contempt we have for our past and the selves we once were, I tell the boy. The vista from my window, which I always contemplated while the flavored water boiled on the stovetop behind me, well I have yet to see another prospect I like so much. Perhaps it is not best for one's health to drink two hot liquids one so soon after the other, I have no idea. I lived by my wits then, soaking up information where I found it and applying it somewhat drunkenly. How often I would stand by my window repeating a word like effluvium until it became nonsensical.

A cough. I look over my shoulder. Edmund's brother lies splayed on the ground like a dropped thing. Look at the chaos humming away down there, how amazing it is, I say, jabbing my thumb at the city. The boy does not move. Glove buyers know nothing of a spot like this, I tell him. Remember, they need every prospect labeled. Immediately as I say this, I notice, next to the boy's arm, yes and again a few feet away: litter. No mistaking it. Two cigarette ends, a bottle cap. Sweet Mary, I murmur, getting to my feet, But I am quite wrong. Pivoting, I see scraps of newspaper bearing traces of faded ink and impaled on the tree's branch, a ghostly plastic shell, empty of its popular potato snack. Oh, I say, turning slowly, Oh, oh, oh, but I am very wrong. This is not a spot, after all. Do you see this litter? These dented cans of sugary liquid? Do you know what this is? I ask. The boy continues to lie completely still; for a moment I wonder if he might have quietly expired. Hey! I say loudly, Do you know what this is? He shakes his head without lifting it. This is a *View*. It is a shame you have left behind your green notebook, I say, lighting a cigarette, Because I have yet to see a clearer example of what I call a *prepared moment*. There it is! I say, pointing to a bench I did not see until now, The bench! My god, I say, shaking my head in sorrow, How ideal this view is for the glove buyers of Rome. I hate Views, as you know, I tell him, Views are for people who need direction and we need none. The boy lifts his head. Aren't we going to the zoo? he says. In a minute, I say, coughing. As you know, I hate prepared moments, but, far more than prepared moments, I hate the glove buyers who must talk about experiencing those moments. This is a sluttish view before us, I warn the boy, pointing. This view has tangled with countless viewers. We are not content to be the thousandth lover of a view, we must be the first, or at most the second lover of a sight. True, I continue, This view of our city is not a massive slut like the Forum or the Sistine Chapel, those are sluts of epic proportions. I return my gaze sadly to the city roofs, Yet, by God, this view is still a slut. The boy grunts to show he understands me. We must find beauty where no one has found it, that is the operation, I say. One that becomes more and more difficult. I wager even Hell is clogged with tour buses. We will arrive in that fiery place expecting to be the first to discover its beauty only to find it echoing with clamors for fried dough.

The boy sits up, interested. Is that what sort of food they have in Hell? He asks, Fried dough? Hm, I say, exhaling smoke, Good point. I suppose it's more likely they have no food at all in Hell. Or perhaps they eat vegetables down there; I have no idea. In any case, Hell might be spoiled but there are other possibilities, different ways to locate beauty. We continue to look or we die. My words ring out. An echo somewhere. We continue to try or we are dead. And don't be fooled by reinterpretation, I warn, You must steel yourself against falling for the reinterpreters of the world. A reinterpreter will betray you in an instant. He presents an image as fresh when in fact the image is stale and the language is fresh. Betrayal is the very worst of sins, don't you agree? I ask the boy, We must guard ourselves against betrayal. Against beauty. And against love. Fine, Edmund's brother says. You understand? I ask. He nods. We stare at each other. I lift my chin and narrow my eyes. He nods again, more eagerly. Fine, I say. On to the zoo.

We hurry from the viewing spot, brushing at our clothes to rid ourselves of any souvenirs. Down the hill we storm quite refreshed from our observations. Above, the sky remains cloudless and sun-brightened, ignorant of how its pretty rays are constantly damaged by reinterpreters the world over. We only judge how the sun damages us, I say, But think of the damage we inflict on the sun with our obsessive reinterpreting. But the boy is not listening. He has his elbow pulled around to his chin and is staring at it intently. I watch him weave across the street. He stops suddenly and looks up. Wordlessly I motion that he might step off the street and onto the pavement. He obeys my silent instruction without missing the opportunity for a hop.

I wonder why it is you find the exploration of your body so fascinating, I muse. If it isn't the excavation of your nose, it's the scratching of your head or the picking at your knee. I don't stand here for my own benefit, I tell Edmund's brother. I don't speak simply because I like the sound of my own voice, I say, though I happen to have an extremely pleasant voice and many people have pressed me to consider working on the radio. I am standing here that you may learn the things it has taken me many years to discover, I say. If you think it's been a blessed fun-fair ride learning the things I've spent a lifetime learning, you are wrong my friend, very wrong. Does this look like the face of an angel? I ask, making a circling motion with one finger. Because I didn't gain these scars from staring at my elbow when I could have been learning a lesson. In truth, my scars are barely visible, unless I am scrutinized under a powerful light in which case a few are visible. Edmund's brother watches me patiently, waiting for me to finish. Well what is it? I ask. The boy points his elbow at me. Splinter, he reports. I look at his elbow, confused. I thought you wanted to go to the zoo, I say. The whole damn day is being poured down the drain. The boy bites his lip. But it hurts, he says. Alright, I say, Let's take a look. Indeed, there is a fat splinter shining through the boy's pale skin. Easy enough, I say though I fear blood like a cat does water, not my cat who liked nothing more than to jump into my bath, but most other cats. If the boy starts to bleed I will become short of breath and sick to my stomach. Though it is unlikely I will vomit since I never care to, on the whole. I look around for a pin of some kind. Nothing sharp. I try pressing the skin around the splinter to see if I might persuade it out that way, but the boy's harsh squeal is so painful to my ears that I immediately stop. It seems the zoo will not receive our attentions on this day.

And so we return to our rooms.

Imagine what Edmund will say when he discovers we have spent the entire day learning absolutely nothing, I tell Edmund's brother as I search the kitchen for a pin. The boy straddles a yellow chair, studying his splinter. But we couldn't find the zoo, he murmurs as I go down the corridor, How can we learn anything if we can't find the damn zoo in the first place? I remove a straight pin from the hem of my blue dress and double back. Now hold on just a minute, I say, regarding him from the doorway. While it is true that Rome's famous zoo eluded us this afternoon, we learned other things, did we not? Any mental defective can ogle locked-up animals; how many children are fortunate enough to receive what we call a *life lesson?* Edmund's brother considers. Not many? he asks. Exactly right, not many, I confirm. And don't say damn. Then I hold up the pin, letting it glint in the light. Are you ready? The boy nods, eyeing the glittering pin. Don't be frightened, I say. I'm not, he tells me, jutting out his lip. Where shall we operate? I ask, sticking the pin into my sleeve for safekeeping while I review our options. I dart into the front room. No, no. I return, dumping our breakfast things in the sink. The kitchen will serve as our operating theater. In truth I am beginning to relish the idea of surgery. Up you go, I say, smacking the table with my palm. This day began like any other, yet thanks to the boy I am living out a childhood dream. Oh yes, in those days before Edmund or my husband, when I believed my whole life lay open to me, I had a small dream to one day practice surgery. For certain reasons that desire never came to pass. But now, on this rather ordinary day, I am living out that dream without the effort or cost of a medical degree. I instruct the boy to lie on his back, right hand gripping left shoulder the better to access his elbow. Then I scrub my hands at the sink, holding them up in front of me, as I have seen the best doctors do. If only I had an obsequious nurse and a waiting room full of patients hanging on my every word. What's taking so long? the boy asks. I wipe my hands dry on my dress and pluck the pin from my sleeve. Usually you want antiseptic in these procedures, I say, But all I have is soap so in this case it will be soap we use. The boy stares at the pin. Hold on, I say and go for the scotch. As a girl I was given scotch-soaked cotton for toothaches and I cannot smell the stuff without instantly feeling a pain in my gums. This is known as a Pavlovian effect, I tell the boy as I pour a tumbler for him to drink, my gums smarting like hell just from the stink. As he sips the anesthetic, I lecture him, both on the many forms of anesthesia and on Pavlov's notions of dogs. The unfortunate result of which is that I do not see him refill his cup with more scotch as I am racing back and forth across the room on all fours the better to demonstrate Pavlov's maxim. When I see the little monster knocking back the scotch with an expert flick of his head, I snatch the cup and throw it in the sink. Finally everything is in order. I hover over his arm, debating the merits of where to begin. Edmund's brother lifts his head. His face has turned a rather nasty color. Is it out? he asks. I have yet to touch him. Nearly, I say. In truth I am suddenly quite worried about the boy's health. I was so enjoying my parody of a Pavlovian puppy, I have no idea exactly how much scotch the child has swallowed. There is a good chance I will have to prompt a vomiting. I rarely like to do so since I am unable to vomit myself. I have never liked things propelled by unknown forces to make their way through my body in the wrong direction. I tear a small thread in his elbow above the splinter. With a conviction that arrives in times of urgency, I hook the pin under the splinter and begin to work it out. Oh yes I am very confident. You wonder why I diligently watch the surgeon, the butcher, why I track the movement of hand and arm, the set of the hip, the purse of lips. Because it is all in the body, not the head as so many mistakenly think. If one can master the choreography, the vocation will come. When I apprehend the boy's splinter, I narrow my eyes like the doctor of my aunt. After proclaiming me exceptional, my aunt took to her bed and set about dying of emphysema. I bestowed her with grapes even as she foundered, scrawping at the covers like a crow. Because I knew no better. Her doctor, Dr. Hannich with a hard K ending, always narrowed his eyes when he looked at her chart or lifted her gown, which he did often, often I mean for a doctor investigating chest problems. But this is getting away from me; what an ill portrait of Hannich I paint when I embarked on his squint. All this time I'm still on the boy's splinter, narrowing my eyes to better the extraction as Hannich himself would have done. He whom I called with a soft sound to his name, as if he were a verb when he was most certainly a noun. But I noted his manner, his body and its movements quickly, even at thirteen. I was astute then, but less of life had beaten me. I stood by clutching my sweaty grapes as dear Hannich stooped to investigate my aunt. The doctor was puppet-like in many ways. I understood then as I understand today that the higher degrees conferred in education are contingent on bad posture and a cold glittering eye. The body, the body, need I say it again, what peril to ignore its will. Although my body despises me for its inability to speak and seeks its revenge in a variety of crippling pains, though we have an uneasy friendship at best, more of a détente I would say, still I respect the theater my body needs. My body knows things my brain has no idea about. In another minute the splinter lies in my palm. It was Dr. Hannich's squinting of course, I could not have done it were I just myself. Prostrate on the table, the boy has fallen asleep. Or blacked out. This is not the

day I had in mind for us, I say, lifting him in my arms and stag-
gering down the corridor. This is not the ordinary way to educate little boys.

I set the boy down on his bed. His body is so limp it is more
the pouring of a liquid than the setting down of a solid. I light a
cigarette and try to drum up some medical facts. Something
should be elevated, feet or head. It is now nearly two o'clock,
the day has been monstrous since its aurora. The boy will grow
ignorant of the differences between fauna, he will mistake frogs
for toads, and the fault will lie with me. He had a chance at a
real kind of life; now that chance has gone and no doubt I will
be caring for him at fifty. The boy's miniature mouth moves in
some sort of dreamspeak. There are surging pangs that run
through me sometimes. I imagine it is the feeling you have before sailing off a cliff on a machine built for that purpose. Perhaps it is the feeling some women have toward their husbands,
I don't know, I never had any surgings for my husband. My
memory is that he tipped his cap at me the day we met, though
I don't recall my husband ever wearing a cap. He took an hour
every morning to attend to his hair; it would have been eccen-
tric to spend so much time arranging the sweep of his forelock
only to smash a cap down on it. I may have seen a film once
where a man tipped his cap. Perhaps I am so desirous of being
the object of a cap-tipping that I simply adapted the film to my
own history. These are the mysterious forces that roil below our
surfaces that have us hearing things people did not actually say

or reading minds that are in fact blank. In any case, it was only a matter of days before my husband was making deposits and withdrawals in my rooms and soon enough that he was insisting on a dusty rose color for my wedding trousseau. In those days I never argued or answered back and I would often find myself in places uncertain as to how I had arrived, new towns for example or a strange restaurant or dance hall or, in this instance, at my own wedding. The habit disappeared not long after I was married. In the months and years between my wedding day and the day I left my husband, I never found myself places accidentally. While I was with my husband I had my eyes wide open, as a married woman must, and I was the initiate of my own journeys, tepid as they were, often consisting only of the treacherous route from kitchen to bedroom. At the wedding I knew the whole dismal affair would end horribly; I predicted bloodshed when I saw the cake. It was grey and shapeless; where I had hoped for something white with piped roses. There was no family for either of us, his had perished operatically, mine had drifted into death. The pink dress had an oily sheen, my husband would not allow a white dress; he preferred to suggest my compromised character.

What a funny word, marriage. I see the grey cake, the collection of housecoats in the closet. He married me and I began to decompose. I used to run into town while my husband was at work. Smoking cigarettes with the girl who sold us eggs, visiting the piano teacher or the bread man who threw me fresh pastries I ravaged with my teeth all the way home. My husband developed a tuneless whistle, easy in his observation that he had saved me from a life of drudgery. If there's anything I hate it's being saved. My husband on the other hand liked to save young women as well as bitten dogs or recalcitrant horses. We had to shoot the bitten dog shortly after saving him. You can see the parallels without me having to draw them. Being saved puts me in a foul mood, this is the mood I brought into my marriage and the only thing I took with me when I left, besides a great deal of cash. I blew the entire sum at the Alpine Inn, a gesture that was unbalanced at best. It was there that I met Edmund and he is where our story begins.

As you know, I tell the boy as we walk to the butcher's, I met your brother at the strangest place ever invented. This place was in the Alps, those mountains that greedily appear in so many nations. I wore my buckle shoes that night, I say, The very same shoes you love to buckle for me today. You can imagine the impression those shoes made on your brother, on that weak heart of his. The boy walks slowly, yawning. After sleeping for an hour he is yawning still. Perhaps the whiskey has not entirely left his system. We pass an elderly woman who has stopped to watch birds cross the sky. Good day, she says without looking at us. And the same to you, I reply with a little bow. We continue on our way. I have no patience for old people, I tell Edmund's brother, We never had old people in my family and without early introduction to such things irrational fears can take hold. Everyone fears something, I continue. Spiders, heights, and in my case, the aged. Yes, I say, Walking death. The boy nods and promptly collides into a streetlamp. Ow, he says, backing up and rubbing a spot on his head.

I take out a cigarette and light it. I'm sorry you did that, I say quietly, That certainly looked painful. He does not stop rubbing his head. Here's a question, I say, Are you walking with your eyes open? Edmund's brother looks up at me from under heavy lids. He nods. I'm just wondering, I say, Because that streetlamp has been there for about two hundred years, certainly it has been there the entire time we have been walking down this street. The boy blinks slowly. I didn't see it, he murmurs. I gaze at him over my cigarette. Are you drunk? I ask suddenly. He rolls his eyes. I'm quite serious. The last thing we need is for your brother to think we spend our days at the bottle. Is your vision impaired? I ask, fluttering my fingers near the corner of his eye. The boy jerks his head away. Don't, he says moodily. What about your ears? I say, looking around for something to smash. We are standing on a sidewalk in the residential district; there is nothing to smash. So I bark. Once, loudly. The boy jumps. So far so good. Can he touch his finger to his nose? He can. Can he walk a straight line? As well as he can walk it sober. Fine, I say. We will go buy some meat, we will return to our rooms to fry that meat for your brother and we will act very serious and very sober. Understand? The boy nods. Good, now let me smell your breath. He leans forward, opens his mouth and breathes. I sniff. Not scotch, but something I cannot place. Fine. Onward, I say, taking his hand.

　　We cross Via Maddalena. At the top of the street the hoary woman disappears through a doorway. She has watched all the birds she needs to watch this evening. We are nearly at the butcher's, I tell the boy. What was I saying before we stopped? Something important? This is a trick question, as the boy well knows. The Alpine Inn? He says cautiously. Aha, I say, Exactly right. Now your brother sat by the fire with a group of bores, I continue, What choice did I have but to save him? The boy squeezes my hand. There was a woman, he says, In a white dress. Quite right, I say. Edmund was talking to a beautiful woman in a white dress. If this were a fairy tale, she would be a princess and everything would work out well for her; in the end she would get some sort of crown. However because this is my story the princess gets left behind. We arrive at the butcher's. Edmund took you home instead of her, the boy says. I open the door for him. That's right. So never let it be said your brother has made no sacrifice, I say, though in fact I say so all the time. Hanging from my hand, the boy sticks his shoe in a crevice in the wall and thinks about that for a minute. Your brother's friends did not stop their conversation when we walked away arm in arm, I tell the boy as we wait for the butcher's attention, They made obscene nudging movements with their elbows like inferior comics. I might have returned to my room that night, to my companion and my reading matter. Had this been the case I would know what follows *Call me Ishmael*. As we stand here together in the butcher's shop, I would know who the hell Queequeg is and what Melville meant by his boggy soggy squitchy picture, his grand ungodly god-like man. It is possible that today I could be a scholar had I not met Edmund. But do I lecture panting acolytes on Melville's hidden games? I ask Edmund's brother, No, I do not; I humble myself for pig knuckles. This is what we call life. And we have no more life than we have at this moment.

Edmund arrives home earlier than usual. We are in the kitchen; I am frying onions, the boy sits in a yellow chair drinking milky tea. Hello, Edmund calls from the front door. We are surprised to hear him; it is only half past the hour. I drop the spoon I am using to stir the onions and turn to the boy. He is already tugging at the white bandage I tied around his elbow. Together we manage to rip the thing off just as Edmund appears in the kitchen doorway. In a flash I have the bandage hidden behind my back; the boy doubles over in a coughing fit. Edmund looks from me to his brother then back to me again. What are you up to? he asks. The boy shakes his head, still coughing. Up to? I ask. Edmund smiles, walks over to me and puts his arms around my waist. Good evening, he says and kisses me. But behind my back he takes both my wrists, gripping them tightly. Aha, he says, what's this? He wrestles the bandage from my hands. Nothing, I say. Edmund holds up the white bandage in front of him. What on earth? I grab the bandage from Edmund, blow my nose with it then shove the thing in my décolletage. Just a handkerchief, I say. Edmund looks at his brother. The boy shakes his head, shrugging, Just a handkerchief, he says. You two, Edmund says, turning to take a bottle from the top of the refrigerator. Behind his back I wink at the boy and he blinks back at me, both eyes, opening then squeezing them shut. Edmund takes a glass from the cabinet and pours himself some wine. He sits down, hands on knees, with a sort of groan. The boy returns to his scribbling. Well, Edmund says, studying his brother, I certainly hope you learned something today. Naturally, I say. The boy puts down a red pencil and picks up a blue. Marriage is a tomb, he recites. I spin around, dropping the spoon again. I beg your pardon? Edmund says, Marriage is what? I stare at the boy. The brother stops scribbling and looks up. Love is fatal? he asks. We learned about *animals,* I correct, bending for the spoon. During our bus ride home that afternoon I lectured at some length on the slow-moving ways of the elephant, the tall neck of the giraffe. Of course it is quite possible that the boy absorbed not a word he was so taken by his elbow. That's right, we learned about animals, the boy amends. I smile. Then he adds, At the zoo. And I stop smiling. The boy flashes a brazen grin. He knows I cannot bear fibbery; the gentlest of lies is enough to make my blood boil. The zoo? Edmund says, What, the Bioparco? I turn back to my onions. Inside I am thinking, *the damned Bioparco.* Edmund's brother taps his pen on the table. We saw elephants and a giraffe, he says, And dogs. Dogs? Edmund says, swallowing, Surely they don't have dogs at the Bioparco? I am shocked to hear how easily the boy lies; I should put a stop to it immediately. They had seventeen dogs, Edmund's brother says, At least seventeen, maybe more. On the other hand, there may come a time in the boy's distant future when his life hangs on a lie, if for example bandits have kidnapped him and are about to drip water on his head for several days. In such a situation it will serve the boy if he is able to lie like an expert. And if the boy is to learn to lie expertly, he must do so with my supervision. Of course the ethics of lying, the when and where must also be learned, but at some later date. I set down sausages and onions as Edmund's brother tells Edmund all about the dogs at the Bioparco. Next I hear him tell of the tiger's striped coat and fanged jaw, the cold-blooded habits of the alligator. Between them I sit eating the spongy meat. Back and forth they go until I cannot feel my face. Of course, I say suddenly, clearing my throat, There are many factions that believe it is beyond cruel to keep an animal locked in a cage. Edmund and his brother look at me; their faces turn confused. Can you imagine how bored the snake must be to have his mice thrown at him by some bored roué instead of stalking his prey in the wild? Does it occur to you how depressed those lions are, lolling around waiting for hamburger to be thrown at their bored faces every day at half past six? I'm surprised any animals remain at the Bioparco given that they must be bored to death sitting in a cage all day with a few slim trees. It's difficult to believe the Bioparco animals didn't stage a revolt a long time ago. Can you really think that being stared at by a group of round pink faces is any way to live? Edmund's brother stares at his fork, dragging it through the onions. I push my plate aside. Hey, Edmund says, Hey. I get up to find a cigarette. Listen, I say, You have placed me in charge of this one's education and it is imperative to know all sides to the story. We like to take the good with the bad, am I right? I turn to the boy. He shrugs. Have I traumatized you? I ask. The boy shakes his head. There, I tell Edmund, You see. Mercy is part of a well-rounded education.

Poor Edmund was plucked from school at fourteen to join his father selling useless trinkets door to door. I light my cigarette and lean against the sink, inhaling deeply, looking from one to the other. I don't like to assert my educational superiority over Edmund, but sometimes there really is no choice. Sometimes Edmund pushes me into a position where I am forced to remind him exactly which of us has the benefit of an advanced education. To my knowledge Edmund has never won a prize of any sort. As far as I know prizes have never been dispensed to slow thinkers. Of course, slow thinking may be a virtue somewhere on the globe, I have no idea.

Can't the boy go to the zoo in peace? Edmund asks quietly. I laugh. Well now, who's not giving the boy any peace, hm? I ask. Not me, that's for certain. As far as I'm concerned the boy has peace from sunup to sundown. But I insist on truth as well as peace, I add. As long as I'm responsible for his education the boy will know the truth about things, however dark that truth may be. The boy stands and takes his plate to the sink. In my day we used to go to the zoo to look at the animals, Edmund says. Then buy something sweet to eat. We watch the boy walk back to the table, pick up the other two plates and carry those to the sink. You know how I feel about sweets, I say, You know the havoc sugar wreaks on the teeth. Edmund's brother drags a chair to the sink and climbs up on it. The zoo is not simply the zoo, I tell Edmund, Much as you would like to believe otherwise. Edmund takes out his cigarettes; they are lethally strong and smell like a barnyard. He takes one from the packet and taps it on the table. Well, he says pleasantly, My mistake. And here I thought the zoo was just the zoo. He stands, lights his cigarette and walks out. The muscles in his back dance beneath his work shirt. Edmund.

The brother is squeezing dish soap over the plates in mad curlicues. I pull on a pair of bright pink gloves. Together we douse and scrub the dishes. We name the capitals of various countries, what we can remember of their imports and exports. Afterward I help the boy into his sleepthings and we talk of the many things we might do tomorrow. We might for example find a different language to learn; we might need to have another look at the river. I wish we never had to go to Toby's again, the boy says softly as he falls asleep. Someday, I whisper, We will have all the money in the world, then we won't be forced to take our coffee from people who hate to wash. Don't worry, I promise and I pull the covers over him and switch off the light.

In our bedroom, Edmund has drawn a chair up to the window. He appears to be painting a pear and an apple on the windowsill. I look from him to the canvas to the fruit. Then that triangle again in the other direction. Edmund clinks his paintbrush in a jar of muddy water. Are you *painting*? I ask. He does not look up. I've never seen you paint, I say, I had no idea you were some sort of artist. Still nothing. I could pose for you, I offer, sinking into the mattress, Many artists painted trollops. Edmund studies the fruit fixedly. Not that I'm a trollop, I add. Silence. I get up and walk around him to survey his work. That's the frame of the window bending there, am I right? I ask after a moment. Edmund nods. You'll want some yellow, I advise, To distinguish the foreground from the background. Otherwise there's no dimension, I say. Carefully Edmund rinses his brush. I lean in front of him, stretching to pluck his coat from the floor. I take the coat to the cupboard, brushing off the sleeves. Of course I was never very accomplished at the arts, I say, Though I excelled at other things. History, for example. Oh yes, I knew all the dates. Even today I see most things in terms of the past. The revolutions, damage done in the name of empire, the pillaging, I excelled at that. They gave me a prize naming me best in school, I tell Edmund. Funny the extent to which I hate old things, given that I won our history prize. The fussy buildings in this city make me sick, I say, shaking a cigarette from its packet. Our bedroom window faces a brick wall but I go to it thoughtfully as if I mean to assess the architecture. When your brother first came to us I brought him to museums. One after the next we dutifully worshipped the precious things under glass but the entire time I had to restrain myself from jumping out the window. God the tedium of all that age. When who gives a damn, really. Edmund wipes his hand on his trousers. Don't get paint on your clothes, I tell him, Or I'll never get it out. Fine, he says. What do you think it means to excel at something that interests one so little? I ask, It's a special kind of hell, don't you think? Edmund shrugs. I look back at the bricks opposite. Perhaps I could have parlayed my gift into a sideline of some kind, archeology for example or antiques. Archeology might have been interesting, I say. But hot, I add. Where I can see the appeal of a great discovery, a shroud of Turin or a Rosetta stone, for the most part archeology sounds unbearably hot, not to mention filthy. As you know, I remind Edmund, I am clean to the point of fanaticism. Imagine me sweating in some old desert. Edmund says nothing. Imagine all that perspiration staining my dresses. That must be why I never became an archeologist, I murmur. That's undoubtedly why, Edmund agrees quietly. His face is very white and bland, his mouth set in a line as if he has zipped it. Sometimes I want to bash his face in. Sometimes I find myself casting around for a wide plank. I am bored to the brink of sadism. Edmund wipes his hand on his trousers. With a cowy smile he looks from the fruit to his canvas then back to his still life again. This place is like a cave, I say finally. Edmund looks up. If I enjoyed living in a dark sour place I might just as well have stayed with my husband, I say. Edmund reaches forward to make a minute adjustment to his still life. I stub out my cigarette and immediately light another one. I wonder what you would do if I left, I say. Imagine waking in the morning to find the bed empty. Wouldn't that be a shock? Then you could lug your brother around like some blessed Saint Christopher and I could . . . Edmund looks up at me, cocking his head and raising an eyebrow like a spaniel. You could what? He asks. Well, I could do whatever I like, I say. I might go back to working in a bank as I did before I was married. I might return to school and take a degree or two. There are many things I could do, hundreds of choices I might make. It might surprise you to find there are a thousand aspects in the world besides this brick wall. Edmund gets up. Is that so? he says. It is, I tell him. He walks around behind me and puts his arms around my waist and leans his chin on my shoulder. He reaches around the front of me and unfastens my top button. I'm leaving you, I say miserably, watching his hands. He moves to the next button. Yes, he murmurs, Of course you are. No really, I tell him, I am. To a place you will never find me. No, he whispers in my hair, Don't do that don't leave. I may, I say, encouraged, I very well may. And you won't find me perished on the floor of some river with stones in my pockets. You will find I have become more successful than you ever dreamed. I might found a movement. You might find I've exceeded your expectations. Edmund moves his head to the other side of my neck, kissing it, pulling up my hair to get at every place on my neck. Come on, now, he says. Come on. His hands move to my waist. Wouldn't you miss me? he murmurs. I lean against him. Never, I say. My hand rests on his belt. Edmund, I say. And his hands are everywhere at once, unbuttoning my dress, on my face, turning me to him, confusing me in a blur of hair and hands. And we fall together on the bed. Maybe I'll leave first, Edmund murmurs into my neck, Maybe I'll be the one to go. He is moving slowly now, pulling off my stockings, one by one. My hands grip his neck. That's a far better idea, I say. Make your way into the famous countryside you're always talking about. Edmund stands, pulls off my shirt, says, Shall I? Leans over me. Shall I? he murmurs in my ear. Yes, I say. Go.

I have lain awake for hours watching Edmund sleep, memorizing the notches on his spine. I have smoked in the kitchen and stood at the living room window staring down on the piazza. I have stretched out on the bristled carpet in the living room and sat at the kitchen table dealing cards over and over.

In the boy's room I watch him sleep; I smoke and stare out of the window. On the street a man in a hat stops, looks from side to side, then begins to walk again. For a moment I thought that was my husband, I tell the boy quietly, But now I see my mistake. My old husband had a very particular way of walking, a

lopsided shuffle I have since noticed in a number of his coun-
trymen. In the beginning I was smitten by my husband's singular pace but soon I grew to loathe it, as we often find ourselves
hating the things that once moved us. Of course on these occasions it is really ourselves we hate, I murmur, Our own stupid
youth we find so hateful. As I stand here at your window I find
the memory of my husband's special walk moves me again. My
old husband cared for me very much, I say, In truth I am
amazed he has failed to give chase. But he may not have survived me leaving, in particular the way I left, which was both
sadistic and inventive. I tried to reason with him but in the end
I just left. This is the way I am, I add in a glowering sort of way,
Unpredictable. Although he is asleep, Edmund's brother
should understand exactly how tentative his whole situation is,
how I might up and leave at any moment for I have the will of
the wild birds, I am that unpredictable. Frankly I am astonished my husband has not sent detectives on my trail for he was
a very rich man, I tell the boy, though in fact my old husband
was only moderately rich and could not, for example, seem to
hire a man to clear the rats from the swimming pool. My husband will find me some day though it may take time. When he
does find me, I say, I don't expect that he'll kill Edmund,
though he may try. It might be a matter of weeks before we
see my old husband trot up this alley, but we must be patient.
We must bide our time, I say, though I suddenly cannot recall the
meaning of the word bide. It could be that I hate to bide; I have

no idea. Biding things might be unbearable, with time the most horrific of all. Bide could be a synonym for some sort of torture with sharp metal spikes and terrible things shoved under the fingernail. We must be patient, I amend firmly. It boggles the mind that given the choice, my husband turned to me instead of Samina, with her cunning pots of yogurt and well-pressed shirts. He may well have been a masochist, I will never know. Back when I first lived with my husband I used to smoke under an umbrella by the pool, I tell Edmund's sleeping brother. The umbrella was festooned with a string of cloudy lightbulbs most of which had burned out; a few of which hesitated blue, a tired green from time to time. The swimming pool I stared into as I sat under the umbrella was quite empty. Empty of water I mean; on occasion a rat or two would race back and forth in a state of quandary and in autumn you could count on finding a good ten inches of leaves, so you see *empty* is not an apt description of this pool though it held no water. By its side I sat, smoking, watching my fingers become increasingly yellow, raising a hand languidly to swing the hanging bulbs above my head. I tell you this, I tell the boy, In order that you will gain some understanding of the situation I left, why I was forced to make a break for it and head for the Alps. You see, I say, Even after only a few months at my husband's compound I found that everything looked the same, sounded the same, in fact was all flatly the same. Nothing was ravished with change and mutation, the sky was merely the sky. And I surmised that this state applied not just to my husband's compound and that filthy pool, but to the entire world. I could think of no place I would rather be, no place that could hold anything more interesting than an empty swimming pool. I was dying, you see.

Then one day as I sat outside making the colored bulbs swing, I remembered something, how or why, what brought the image to mind is difficult to say, but I recalled quite clearly a time when it had all been so different. There she was, the girl in the bank, taking lunch on her favorite bench, watching a cannibalistic pigeon peck a chicken bone. How thrilling to find in a pigeon his pigeon properties, to admire his green throat and suspicious eye as if it is your first pigeon. Oh she threw back her head and laughed and laughed, this girl. Yet here I was, not much older and suddenly no different from a rat running back and forth in a swimming pool. Except that I had a cigarette. The memory of the girl I had been suddenly drove me insane and I jumped to my feet, ducked under the bulbs and started to pace. I even tossed aside my cigarette. This was unfortunate since it landed in some leaves in one corner of the swimming pool and started a small fire. In a flash, with more verve than I had shown in years, I leapt into my husband's pool and began to stomp. Stomping, stomping, stomping, once I liked to live, yes, yes, once I had it once, the ardor of the poet, the eye of the photographer, and through my mind again and again, lashing like a cat-o'-nine-tails, was the idea that I had once found beauty where some would swear none existed. I don't think I chanted as I stomped but the impulse was certainly there. Meanwhile the poor rats were becoming quite unhinged by the stomping and began to panic, skittering and jumping wildly, fearing for their lives. I wanted to burn up; I wanted to disappear in flames. When my husband returned home that night, I could barely look up. I pushed some limp green matter around a pan and smoked several cigarettes as he talked about his husband things. I blamed him, who wouldn't. He had taken a girl from a bank and forced her into a kind of slavery. True, my husband never asked anything of me and certainly provided many niceties. But niceties have seldom moved me much. I set down the food and watched him chew, skeptically, cheerfully, my husband in his little mustache and cap. As he ate, I tried to scrape the yellow stain from my fingers. It cannot be removed, that yellow stain that comes from too much nicotine. As I scrubbed the stain it came to my intelligence that there was a great deal of chewing in the room and since I was not eating, that left my husband doing enough chewing for several people. That was my husband for you, or as luck would have it, for me. Chewing and chewing, the man would fall down dead before venturing that the greens were improperly cooked. Did you have a nice day? he asked between chews. I fail at everything I attempt except the slow withering of my appetites, I told him in a joshing way. At one time my husband laughed at the silly things that came from my head. That evening, he watched me silently as he swallowed some wine and I winced as a largish lump worked its

way down his esophagus. Oh husband, how sorry I am, in looking back, at the wretch I was then, though in truth it is likely I
am no better now. Thinking only of escape, I brought his plate,
the plate of my husband as they phrase it in some languages, to
the sink. Behind me my husband may still have chewed on something needing his mastication. He may still be chewing to this
day. I do not know. I believe had I ever worn glasses I would not
have worn them then, not by the pool, nor by my husband. That
was my feeling, why? Because I did not want to see or because
things were better blurred. Or because things were taken from
me at that time, yes taken or robbed, hijacked or extruded; I did
not want to see what I was losing. All this I thought in my dotted
lines from sink to table, from pool to bedroom. All this went
through my mind while I planned my escape, roaming the compound for any final images to store away. After all, it could be that
my husband's compound was unusually interesting and I simply
could not grasp it at the time. If this was the case, I wanted to
have memories to examine should my appetite ever return. I do
not like to be denied things; I hate self-denial of any kind. I like
things. I like to have them and the more things the better. As I
watched the rats scamper, it occurred to me that I might never
recapture the glory of that young girl in her bank days. A lack of
spiritual appetite could well be a part of growing older but I
would make the best efforts a person damned by laziness can
make in order to disprove that idea. Surely somewhere I could

find a sight to gladden my heart. And so it came to pass that I found myself in the Alps. It was at this time of course, I say, That I met your brother.

I look over at the boy. Something plugs his breathing slightly. He is a very small boy. I wonder whether he might actually be a dwarf. I have had so little experience with children. I am not entirely certain what is normal for seven. The moon behind me is bright enough that I cast a shadow. I wave and my shadow waves. I wave my hand shadow at the boy to see if he might wake up naturally. If you are in fact a dwarf I won't spend my life tending you, I tell his sleeping form. I am no good at sacrifice; I'll make a hash of it and forget you on a train. I lie down next to him. Apparently you can sleep through anything, I say. My old cat was also a great sleeper; she hated to be woken at any time of day. I learned to wait until that moggy woke naturally before seeking comfort in her pepper-spotted fur. And though natural to you might not include raising two books and slamming them down, I felt it was fair if it appeared accidental. Directly after I first rescued my cat I used to creep up on her and stare, stare with my eyes wide, my face close to hers, willing her eyes to open that I might find comfort in her fat belly and soft fur. She would often feel me there and open one great eye slowly. There was a cruel menace in that eye; it chills me to recall it. For a moment that old cat would stare at me with her one open eye. Then she would close it again even more slowly. By this I was to understand that she was still asleep and her belly unavailable to me at that time. And so we learn. Until I lived with Edmund and could creep to the brother when sleep rejected me, I never knew the relief a human can provide when compared to a cat. I mean no disservice to my cat here, who was a noble creature and stout of heart, if a trifle bow-legged. And if my old husband has not yet set out on my trail, there is a good chance my cat has taken up the task and is trotting through the Alps at this moment, licking at snow to hydrate herself. The boy shifts, kicking at the covers. I wait until he settles, then arrange the covers around him again. I like to crawl into the boy's bed when Edmund mocks me in his happy sleep or, more often, when he curves away from me like an enormous comma parsing some unfathomable sentence. On those occasions I crawl to the boy simply to press my nose into his moist neck and breathe in his strange aroma. Every night I brave the smog of cooking; is it too much to ask the brother to save me from the dread of night, the cold chills that clamp my heart? Is it too much to ask a husband to follow his wife when her head got rattled and she left him in the middle of the night? What if she were deranged, did it not disturb his sleep that she might be wandering the dusty hillocks calling his name, surviving on plants? One bow-legged cat: the sum of my lovers. And let us see how much she loved me should I forget to feed her. As it was, she was terribly fat from all my love. Fat, but with the grace of the fat. No one can dispute that my cat was a noble cat but on this night I need the words no cat can give.

I am leaving now, I'm afraid, I tell the boy, arranging the covers around him though the covers need no arrangement. My time here has come to an end, I say, There is nothing left for me now. Certainly I could remain; I could stay and provide you with the best of my brain but that would leave nothing for me. I understand what this will beget, I say, walking to the window one last time, And I am sorry that your education will suffer under Edmund's tutelage, but I must put myself first for once. I also know that I have stood at the end of your bed and said these things before; I recall those nights, every single one. But this time, my friend, is different. Certainly your brother and I had our fair share of what they call *good times*; I don't dispute that. But as the days have collected under our belts I find his silence bores me to tears. I do not want to wake up one day here in Rome to find myself hypnotized by figurative rats frolicking in their figurative pool. I have done the best a person could to revere the one thing Edmund offered: his back, but now I am ready to leave. I stalk across the room, but at the door find myself slowly turning to face the boy. Don't you see, I whisper, I want to be that girl again, the one on the park bench. The boy continues to sleep soundly. Good-bye, boy, I say finally.

In the kitchen I take Edmund's heavy flannel shirt from the back of a chair and pull it over my dress, buttoning it quickly. Then I slip out the door, closing it gently behind me. A moment later I slip back through the door. From the knife drawer I pull out the soccer photo, wipe off some sticky residue, and place it in my brassiere. Under my arm I have a small knapsack stuffed with my blue dress, a hairbrush, and some lire I found in Edmund's wallet. I have also taken our only map, which I plan to consult in the courtyard before advancing. Hand braced against the dingy wall—the light in the stairwell is dead again—I make my way downstairs and out the back door. By the streetlamp from the alley, a heap of iron deck chairs casts a latticed shadow that breaks and begins again. The bird-bath in the courtyard has gone dry. Tufty grass pushes through the cobbles. I unfold the map and spread it on the ground in front of me. As I bend over it, a packet of Edmund's potent cigarettes falls from the shirt pocket. Smoking one might taste like a kiss. I could use a good kiss right now, yes I could.

I light up, inhale deeply, then stand; I have to be on my way before daybreak. Standing quickly was a mistake. I waver for a moment, spectrally, like a shimmer of heat before I keel over. Every dog, I think as I crumple, Will have its day. Falling is not as painful as you imagine when standing, if you do it properly. Four laundry lines cross overhead like a music staff. Clinging to the middle of one, a disapproving bird moves his head in spastic jerks. You are not fat enough to be a note on my music staff, I tell it. Besides it is night, go find your friends. The bird does not move. It may not be a bird. Please don't shit on me, I say in case it is. Mr. Marcolini has laid the paving stones unevenly, they press uncomfortably into the small of my back and bottom. A breeze slips through my thin nightwear, caressing my thighs

with an icy hand, the sense of burning marbles behind my
eyelids stays as I search the sky. I have not slept for days. An
overlooked pair of lady's underpants hangs solo at one end of
the laundry line. They grieve me, these enormous underpants. I
am imbuing foundation garments with human qualities; I am
finding isolation where there is only cotton and elastic. Lying on
my back, hands cupped to the sky as if it might fill me up. I am
not attached to anything. The world is a great vast place. I close
my eyes. I need to look at the map, find a new place. In a minute.

What are you doing? I wake to a washed-out sun and Edmund's
brother standing over me. Move a step to your left, I say, Block
out the sun a bit, would you? He complies and I lie still for a
minute, catching up to everything. A bird chirps somewhere, a
great mocking chirp. Finally, when I can bear it, I sit up, un-
sticking the matchbook glued to my cheek. What are you doing
out here? the boy says again. I get to my feet. My back feels like
it has been trampled by a horse. Gardening, I say, The weeding
exhausted me. I pick up my bag and start toward the house.
What's that bag for? the boy asks, running after me. Never
mind that, I say, holding out my hand, Let's go upstairs and
watch your brother walk to work. Let's have some milk and begin our day. Perhaps today we won't go see Uncle Toby, how
about that? We could ask your brother for some money that
we might afford a real breakfast in a real café instead of some
hideous train station affair, I say, How about that? We will have

a real day of it; we'll go to the Bioparco today, I tell him, We'll confirm the existence of those dogs you spoke of last night. We have reached the door to our rooms. Edmund's brother twists the knob with both hands. As he does he turns back to me and says, But Edmund's gone. I look down at him, trying to make sense of his words. The boy pushes the door, trips and together we fall into the room with a colossal noise. I land on my wrist, folding it under me. Oh for heaven's sake, I shout. We collect ourselves, swearing, bruised.

This is no way to start the day, I mutter, barging down the corridor and into the bedroom I share with Edmund. I throw open the closet. Edmund's suitcase is gone, as are both pairs of shoes, one black, and an ugly pair the color of moss. Very nice, I say, sinking onto the bed. That's just fantastic, isn't it? Immediately as I descend toward the bed I realize I am going to need to pace. If any situation ever called for a pace, it is the occasion of Edmund's flight. Unfortunately the idea occurs to me exactly as my bottom touches the bed. I have learned by now that I collect injuries when my mind outpaces my body. The one thing I would hate to happen, upon finding Edmund has left us, is to incapacitate myself. I will need all muscles and ligaments in proper working order in the days to come. So I let my bottom settle quite comfortably on the mattress, the mattress that is now mine alone, and I wait for my body to catch up with my mind. The mattress is actually quite comfortable. And I have complained about it so often. I bounce. Then again, with more

vigor. When I am assured that mind and body are one, I get up
and walk to the door. The boy remains in the doorway; by now
he knows the difference between a pace and an exit. So this is
what it looks like to be left, I say, turning on my heel and returning to the bed. This is what my old husband looked like
from the omniscient point of view, I say, How very interesting.
I rub my chin; I look up to the ceiling. I think like a scientist,
sighing as if my experiment has lost its control. In fact my
stomach is pushing at the floor of my lungs, trying to get out.
As I approach Edmund's brother I cluck my tongue as if mildly
aggravated, but on my way to the bed, when my back is to him,
my eyes bulge with pain. Finally I sink back onto the bed. So
now it's just the two of us, I say. Edmund's brother walks across
the room and sits next to me on the bed. Edmund will come
back, he says, taking my big hand in his little ones. Will he? I
murmur, How do you know? Because, the boy says, He just will.
I get up. I would like to tell Edmund's brother that *he just will* is
not an empirical argument, but my heart is not in his education
right now.

In the kitchen I slosh milk into the saucepan and light
the gas. Together we watch the flame lick up the sides of the
pan. And when the milk is hot we watch me pour it into the
bowl. Blow on it, I say, Blow on your milk to cool it, I'll be right
back. In the bedroom, under the chair Edmund sat in last night
while he painted his damn fruit, I find a lone sock. I lie on
the bed with Edmund's sock on my chest like a vestigial foot. I

give myself five minutes. To myself I say, You may take these five minutes to feel the texture of this sock, how it rubs against your hand, five minutes. A clock sits on the bureau; I watch the hand tick past. A soiled white cloth beneath it, saturn rings from spilled drinks. Another minute passes. The night I left my husband, that fat moggy stood, a sentry in my door frame. Four stout legs, solid as a table. The clock does not tick, not audibly or at least not audibly to me. The clock may have a very soft tick, I am not certain, I would not like to say definitely one way or another. There are so few sounds to tell me whether I am losing my hearing. Another minute passes. I hold his sock, after smelling it, desperate for any last traces. But Edmund never had pungent feet. From my mind, those depressing folds, the sound of an aunt wheezing through tubes, the memory of a husband's face souring as he ran the bath. The interesting thing about my time in the Alps, where I fled after abandoning my husband, is that I kept wondering what my husband was doing as I went about my day. As I washed my face I wondered whether he stood or sat at that very moment, or whether he rode his horse though I could not recall my husband ever owning a horse. Then I would stand in front of the mirror for several minutes examining my face without really seeing it, so consumed was I with the idea that my husband ought to have a horse. If everything were as it should be in the world, there could be no logical reason why my father, husband rather, should not have a horse. Poor old husband, whom I treated lamentably, should he not have a high mount from which to look down on the world as he once looked down on me. There was no reason why my slim husband should not be grand and comfortable in his job of looking down on people. No reason at all, I often thought as I stood in front of that bathroom mirror in the Alps, flannel in hand. And suddenly I would come to, I would blink to find myself staring at myself as if I had never seen myself before, as if I were looking straight through myself into unfathomable depths and since I do not possess unfathomable depths, the experience was chilling indeed. Immediately I would throw down the flannel to hurry in search of some sort of salve, which at that time, oddly enough, was gin and bitters.

There's nothing to eat. Edmund's brother stands in the door-way. Morning is now evening. My eyes dart across the ceiling, I cannot let go of Edmund's sock. I pretend I am myopic and make my eyes blur. It's a favorite trick of mine because I have perfect vision. I unblind myself miserably. Holding the sock against my chest, I turn on my side to face the boy. I'm hungry too, I say sadly as if it means something quite different. Maybe we should go to the train station café, he says. I nod. The train station café, I say. Perfect. The train station café.

The café is closed when the boy and I arrive. We see Toby inside, sweeping the floor, so we rap out a tune on the window. Wordlessly, Toby unlocks the door. He looks us up and down, gripping his broom as if he might need to hit us with it at some point. The lights are dimmed; a lone waiter hunches over the bar drinking the last of some whiskey. A half-eaten sandwich lies on a plate in the center of a nearby table. The boy and I ignore Toby: we stare at the sandwich greedily. I believe I see meat spilling from its center but I am uncertain as to what type. I refuse to eat any sort of bird and though the spillage looks too pink to be fowl, I have been known to confuse my colors in times of stress. Toby sighs, and hands the brother the last of his sandwich. Because Toby is not a man who leaves his dependents in the middle of the night, slinking away like a craven dog. No, Toby is a man who gives you the last of his sandwich. If you are Edmund's brother, that is. If you are me, Toby gives nothing. C'est la guerre. Edmund left us, I tell the hunchback in a friendly way as I reach for his whiskey. The hunchback does not raise his head. A broom leans against his side. Everyone has a broom in this place, I say nicely. Light from the café spills onto the sidestreet. I swig at the bottle and stare, mesmerized by the pattern the light makes on the street. The boy is having trouble ingesting the sandwich which looks to be stale. He glances up at me as if I can help him with swallowing. I shake my head. I cannot, I'm afraid. No one has ever depended on me, except my dear cat. And I overfed it. Had the cat burst, it would have been nobody's fault but mine. I am too poor to overfeed the boy, but I could starve him. If I am not careful, I might forget to feed him and he could fall somewhere, some time when I am walking quickly and I might not notice, he might die, all his blood leaking from a fissure, pedestrians passing with little care.

At this point I realize two things. Number one: I am smoking and drinking both. I never both smoke and drink. I do one or the other, never both. Number two: it is not whiskey I am drinking, but rum, which has never been a friend. Number three: I appear to be shouting. I deduce this last based on some swiftly gathered evidence, namely the proximity of the voice to my ear and a gripping sensation in my chest. I appear to be shouting the following: It is my opinion that Edmund cannot accept veneration and I loved his back! If he will not accept love, if he is too fat to accept love, that is no fault of mine. I am getting Edmund mixed up with my cat; the word *fat* is being thrown all over my conversation. The hunchback's broom falls to the floor with a clatter. Love is fatal, the boy declares, We must guard ourselves against love. I turn to him. Yes, I say miserably, I *know* that, I know that. The boy has set the remainder of his sandwich on a table between us. What sort of meat is this, I ask, pointing. Cow, he tells me. Fine, I say, opening my purse. But there is no room for the sandwich because, for whatever reason, Edmund's sock is stuffed in my purse. The boy puts out his hand. I'll carry it, he offers. Fine, I say again, giving him the sandwich, Now let's go. And because I feel drunk and hellish, because I have been throwing around the word *fat,* I decide to get up off the bar stool very carefully. With a renewed grace, I stand slowly. Unfortunately, I am in fact not sitting on a bar stool, my mistake. In any case, I collect myself from the floor quite swiftly and hoist the boy onto my back. I topple a bit from his weight but remain cheerfully upright. There is no need to carry the boy, he has not been drinking, but I appear to be proving a point. Exactly what remains to be seen. Good night, I say, vowing never to speak to Toby again, not if we starve, no, never. Toby jumps up. Wait, he says as I make my way toward the door, a confusing path I venture since there are many windows, several of them large and each one offering likelihood as an exit. Wait, Toby calls again, so that I give up on the exit, drop the boy and turn. Well, what? I ask. Like a cat, not my fat cat, but one with balance, the boy lands neatly on his feet. What is it, Toby? Because I have been watching you for the past *hour*—I am being inflationary, we arrived fifteen minutes ago—And for the past *hour* or so you've really had a laugh at my expense, haven't you? I am suddenly sounding oddly Victorian, as if Toby's behavior has rattled my ancestors. What is it you want, *To-oh-oh-by?* I continue, stretching out his name as if it is an insult. It seems like a night for a tussle, yes, blood spilled, even mine, I can taste it. The rum undoubtedly contains anesthetic properties, it would be nice to see that pretty red color and not even feel it, *To-oh-oh-by?* Toby holds out an envelope. This is for you, he says, holding out a blurry white thing. I focus, narrowing my eyes until I make out . . . an envelope. What's this? I say. He shakes it at me. I take the envelope and rip it open. The three of us watch as bank notes drift to the floor. Money from Edmund, Toby says, flipping a chair up on a table, and then another. Money? The boy, tosses the sandwich onto a table, drops to his knees and begins scooping up the bills. Edmund had to leave Rome, Toby says. Oh, he— really? I say, Do you hear that, little boy? Your brother *had* to leave Rome, notwithstanding that *leaving Rome* is also leaving you and leaving me, not to mention leaving you with me. Toby picks up his broom and resumes sweeping. Why would Edmund leave money here with you instead of in our rooms? Was he so desperate to get out? Petrified that in the minute it took to write a few words he might be caught scurrying through the house like a rat? I ask, Or was Edmund to leave before his brother woke from a nightmare, terrified and in need of a hug? I snatch up the half-eaten sandwich and try to bite it. To my knowledge the boy has never needed or received a hug but Toby is not to know this. Oh, what does it matter, after all, Toby says impatiently, Edmund knew you would come here. Really? I sputter, throwing down the stale sandwich. Is that right? So now Edmund knows things? Suddenly Edmund is a blessed genius that knows every damn thing? Don't tell me now he's intuitive? Now he's a swami shaman of some kind, is it? I am out of breath to such an extent that I am forced to sit and put my head between my knees to coax some blood to my brain. The situation has enraged me and I prefer to be controlled and watchful, like a cat. Not my cat, which was hysterical and skittish, but a different cat, a Siamese I imagine. A minute later, I am right again, upright and quite normal. I can feel the blood throbbing at my temples. I want to scream but I do not. This is what we learn as we shoot up and grow hair in our different parts; we learn not to do the things we would most like to do. So, I turn calmly to Toby. Tell me, why did Edmund leave? Toby shrugs and reaches for another chair but before he can move it, I sit on it. Make a guess, I suggest. Toby leans down next to my ear. Perhaps because you are a hard woman, he murmurs, Perhaps because you have never baked a pie for anyone. I cross my legs. Rubbish, I snap. Toby shrugs and moves to the next chair. So that's your read on it? I ask. Toby shrugs again. Next to us, the boy has begun to sort the bills into piles. There is a great deal of money, more than we need for several weeks. I put my head down on the table. A bill, one with a man's head on it, stares at me. I close my eyes; the rum makes thinking increasingly difficult.

At night I dream of our meeting, how we smashed together. I am back in our Alpine inn, waiting by the bar for a drink. Remember the screech outside, the wild animal at the door and how you snatched my arm, crying out in pain, me there up under your jaw, a place you never expected to find me. I pushed off from the ocean floor; he was a dark shadow of land. My head cracked him on the jaw. What was it I dropped? It was an accident. I wake up panting. The two of us smashed again, tangled together, rolling on the bed fully clothed. Stopping to stare though I could barely make out the shape of his face. We were still clothed. I could feel his hard boot against my naked ankle. I go into the kitchen, stepping over the boy's blocks on the living room floor. I pour myself a glass of water and drink it. In the dark I could feel Edmund's breath, the observance of my features he could barely see. I had the strangest feeling, a wave beginning at my throat. It is no good to think about these things. That night in the Alps we lay together fully clothed, I touched his elbow as if it were a door. Your honor listen to me even as I am here today recollecting and collecting myself, I see him in that photograph edged against the spangled sky. The pain of beauty, don't we outgrow how grotesque it is, how it only lives to torture us. Like one of those boys, I gather at his perimeter, hoping for a view. I am his Boswell, his Leonardo. He will stare back at me from the distant future, gathering his unknowable smile, the landscape dim behind him breathing, swelling. Somehow I sleep again because only a moment later I hear a voice. I sit up quickly. Edmund?

You were screaming.

I fall back onto the bed. It appears to be morning. The boy's hand agitates the doorknob. That sound is so grating, I say. He takes his hand off the knob, but continues to fidget in the doorway. What do you think Toby meant in the café? I ask, examining the ceiling. What did he mean I never baked a pie for Edmund? I raise myself up on one elbow and turn to the boy. Do you think he expected a pie all this time? The boy shrugs. I cooked for you, I say and the boy nods. Hot milk every morning, I remind him, And boiled things at night. Every evening I suffered the stench of cooking for you and your brother and he leaves because I never baked a pie. A pie! When I made all kinds of cooked things in different shapes and colors. Kidney shaped and crescents and mushy brown things that soaked up sauces. *Sopped* up sauces, the boy corrects. Yes, *sopped* up sauces. Remember the pizza? I ask. The boy wrinkles his nose. Okay not the pizza, what about the lentils, remember the lentils? The boy nods vigorously. They were good, he says, crossing to the dressing table. I cooked lentils, I cry, And they were good. So I will not have Toby telling me about pies, I say, I simply will not stand for it. The boy gazes steadily at his reflection. He looks at his profile, then his face straight on. Now his profile again. You see the comments I am forced to suffer from a stinker like Toby? I ask. The boy nods, pulling his fingers through his hair. Toby also said you were a hard woman, he reminds me. Yes, I murmur, pulling out my cigarettes, That's absolutely right, he called me a hard woman, what do you make of that? The boy shrugs again. I light a cigarette. I turn the word over in my mind. A *hard* woman. On the face of it hardness sounds like a very bad thing. A hard woman. Has it ever been good to be a hard woman? Clenching my cigarette between my teeth, I pull back the covers and climb out of bed. I imagine, I say to the boy, exhaling, gathering my shoes, I imagine it is beneficial to be a hard woman if you sled the Arctic. If you manage a team of dogs you have to eat when the food runs out, I imagine then that hardness is a good quality. A soft woman will die if the temperature dips suddenly and she cannot bring herself to skin a dog. In that case the hard woman will triumph. Though if you return to civilization with a brain that cannot bake pies, perhaps hardness is still inferior. The boy freezes. Eat the dogs? he whispers. And what if you are taken captive in enemy territory and forced to survive on fingernail clippings? I ask, I wager only a hard woman survives that, even if she spends the rest of her days left behind like an old sock. Edmund's brother has turned quite white. Did I mishear Toby, I ask, Did Toby in fact say dark, you are a *dark* woman? I wouldn't mind being a dark woman. A dark woman can be mysterious and smutty yet still pliable. Eat the dogs? The boy repeats once more in his smallest voice and I can see I have made a terrible mistake. I clench the cigarette in my teeth and take the boy's hand. Time for milk, I say brightly, Milk time! And we set off down the corridor. Why do people eat dogs? he asks. What on earth are you talking about? I say, No one's eating precious Fido. You *said,* he whines, You *said* a woman eats her dogs in the Arctic. That must have been my dream, I say, You woke me up so suddenly the dreams leaked out my mouth. Let's speak of it no more, I suggest, sloshing milk into a saucepan. The boy sets his mouth in a line. Meanwhile my cigarette has disappeared. I lift up a bowl and some papers on the counter. It's in the milk, the boy says. I fish out the cigarette, now quite wasted, and throw it in the sink. I don't think a hard woman boils milk for a boy who is not her son, I say, That doesn't sound like a hard woman to me. The boy crosses his arms. I am tired of this conversation, he says. I pour milk into his bowl and place it in front of him. Fine, I say, But my final comment is this. I look at him; my mind has turned blank. I have no final comment. Edmund's brother leans forward and blows onto the milk, encouraging it to form a delicious pasty skin.

There's a whole world out there, I tell the boy, Full of many different types. I am gently apprising Edmund's brother of the possibilities of hard women who eat dogs. Some say that ignorance is bliss, I tell him, But it does not follow that wisdom then is misery. I watch the boy blow on his milk, adding stormy sound effects so a tempest brews in his bowl. I decide to say no more on the subject because it occurs to me that though wisdom does not necessarily predicate misery, I have so seldom seen the intelligent joyous. The intelligent, for all my spying, seem fairly depressed as a group, sharing news on the various griefs beneath the moon. Are the stars less wondrous when you can identify what they do up there at night, does the earth become accursed upon discovering the terrible things we visit on it? Difficult to know.

Let's talk about the money, I say, lighting a fresh cigarette, How shall we spend it? I tear off a piece of paper and push it across the table to the boy. Here's a pen, I say, Make a list. You need a suit, I say, Write down Suit. And I need more cigarettes, some stockings and a hat, write down Hat. And a watch and perhaps a dozen handkerchiefs. Perfume would be nice. The boy is staring at me. And a stole of some kind for the cooler evenings, I say, That would certainly be useful. I stare back at him. If you keep your mouth hanging open like that your drool might flood this room. Well, what about *food?* the boy says as if he is speaking to an imbecile. Look at this cash, I say, fanning out the bills, Look at it all. Can't we have some fun? Must we live like wretches until we're found face down in a ditch? What sort of biography is that? A damn dull one if you ask me, I mutter, If you continue on this joyless path, no woman will have you. The boy taps his pen impatiently. But we'll run out of money if you buy all this. You can't have a stole, he tells me, And you don't need a hat. Don't need a hat! Of course I need a hat, everyone has a hat, I say, That old beggar woman on Popolo has a hat, even her donkey has a hat, why am I not allowed a hat? In fact, why have I never had a hat my entire life? Sally had a hat. Samina had a hat, my aunt had a hat, even as she died she wore it in bed. You're wrong, the boy says, Samina never owned a hat. We look at each other. I open my eyes wide, calling his bluff but he won't look away. Stalling for time, I go to the sink. I wash my hands. Then I scrub at the faucet with a filthy rag. Does the boy even *know* Samina? Surely Samina is part of my past and the boy is very much of my present. The past belongs to my husband and my cat, the past before that to Samina and my bank, and the past before that, the most extreme past, belongs to my father and mother, our fire and poor Sally, who was so monstrously scorched. The boy has never known my cat and he has certainly never met Samina. I turn quickly, hoping to catch him blushing from his bold-faced lie. But he is bent over the piece of paper working on the list in that crabbed hand of his. He writes for another minute then holds up the demented list. I snatch it. Milk? Bread? Cheese? I crumple up the paper, throw it in the sink, cross my arms and face him. I used to think I had some kind of life, I tell him, But more and more I find that this is not the case. I find that the old woman who sells rags on Popolo owns a donkey with more life than me, I tell the boy. He is certainly treated better, I say. I am barely alive, I continue, examining my fingernails, I am so near evaporation you could pinch me and I would hardly feel it. Though I advise you not to try, I add quickly. This might not be me at all standing before you, I say, pointing from my feet up to my neck then back to my feet again, All this, it could just be ghostly matter. I might have sloped off this mortal coil a while back and let me tell you it certainly feels like it. What is life, I cry, turning to furiously scrub at the faucet again, I who strove to mark it down, who made it my business to live, live, yes a more fixed, less evanescent life than any other, now finds herself a drab servant with no time for reflection. If you could begin to comprehend the zeal with which I once undertook my search for reverence, it would chill you to the marrow, I tell the boy. I was a racehorse champing at the bit, sizing those around me, wondering, was their veneration better than mine. That was me clawing like a rabid thing to every sound and image. My fingernails bleeding, my breath shallow, eyes wild and roaming, I coursed every room for its layout, what stood where, how it smelled, who looked at whom and what they meant to each other, fixing it in my mind, that was my *job*, I cry, throwing down the rag and sneaking a look at the boy now scribbling idly on the table, To stab each passing moment, to try to understand what comprises a life, what the hell meaning means, to have some bloody faith in something. I never imagined my life would come to this, I say, There is nothing but a fat clock over our heads ticking down the minutes and you deny me a *hat*? I fall into a chair, out of breath, but immensely pleased. After a moment, Edmund's brother gets up, sighs dramatically and retrieves the crumpled paper from the sink. Carefully he smooths out the wrinkles until it meets his fastidious standards, sits back at the table and begins to write. Edmund's brother is not to know that I never let an image corrode my mind. In fact I prefer to lie in bed and let a day's images wash over me in a type of glaze. When I walk into a room I am less likely to fix in my mind the room's design than I am to cast about for signs of a drink. I do not like to feel too much, to see too much. I have read that the world is a noisy place full of curious people, but remarks on its flavorings I leave to others. I just want a hat. The boy hands me the list. The word *hat* has been added below *prosciutto*. Hm, I say, disguising my intense pleasure. A hat. Certainly a hat is a necessity in a city like this. A hat is imperative to separate the classes, I tell him. With a hat we can distinguish the members of our very high class, from the very low class of ordinary people, those we wish to avoid. And what about the donkey? the boy asks, What class does the donkey belong to? I look at him suspiciously but he meets my gaze with frank innocence. Clearly it is not necessary for the donkey to advertise his class, I say carefully, Since everyone can see he is in fact a DONKEY AND NOT A PERSON AT ALL. Then I walk out of the kitchen. I think I will have a felt hat, I call back, Or perhaps one with flowers.

I begin to fashion the ideal hat in my mind as we find our coats, as we count out the money and as we cross the piazza toward the hat section of town. I think about the hat on the bus when I am forced to pull the boy away from petting a blind man's dog. I think about the hat when we jump off the bus and make our way through the crowds to the hat shop. We walk a street of dead people, grey, distracted and dispossessed. The only reasonable reaction is to purchase something at once. You think it's fine, you think it's good, but it's not, it's death. And as we know, only buying some impractical object will stave off feelings of death. In effect you are saying, I fear you not, death, though you hover nearby with your hot breath. In fact, you trouble me so little I believe I will buy myself a hat. Buying a hat, I tell Edmund's brother, Staves off these harbingers of death that surround us.

Exactly at this moment, an enormous woman barges into us, scattering her excitable children, forcing the boy and me to jump off the street and press ourselves into the doorway of a small boutique. Really, the boy says, annoyed. But nothing can annoy me on this day, the day I am at last to have a hat of my own. I hum tunelessly as I search for my hat in the display window. Come on, the boy says, tugging my arm, This is not a hat shop. Wait! I say, stabbing the glass, Look there. Oh my Lord, I murmur, Come to me. The boy looks where I point. That's a pair of sunglasses, he says, not a hat. But I am clapping my hands and pushing open the door before he can stop me. What about death? the boy says, trapping the door shut with his foot, What about staving off death? I shove him aside. Honestly, I say, Must you be so literal? Clearly sunglasses will stave off death as nicely as any hat.

The sunglasses have amber lenses and once I try them on I refuse to take them off. I surprise myself in the mirror, turning away, then turning back with a start, pretending I have happened upon a complete stranger. I look fantastic. It is one thing to be objective, but really. The boy counts out the bills. Fine, but you can't have a hat as well, he says, handing money across the counter. We don't have enough money for both sunglasses and a hat. I don't care, I tell him, tripping, These are so much better than any stupid hat. The glasses have turned the city a startling color between orange and yellow, but then Rome has always seemed jaundiced. If a buffoon like Samina wears a hat, why would I? It strikes me that in order to distance myself from someone as brainless as Samina it is crucial to wear not a hat, but a fantastic pair of sunglasses. You could drag me to my death by horses before you would find me wearing a hat like that slut Samina, I tell the boy. I am in a very good mood. The city is amber; he is going to have a time of it shutting me up. It is all very well to run around shouting about the world's delights, but what about the simple people? I ask the boy over the top of my new sunglasses. What about the laborers? I continue. To some men a field is not a landscape but a plot of dirt they have to plow, what about that? Is a man cursed with a buckling back and seven children supposed to hold up each grain of wheat and crow with wonder? I ask, astonished. We turn to face the river to think about this conundrum. You should write this down, I say, Write it down in your green notebook so you can look at it later. Mention that I hate poetry, I tell the boy as my sunglasses slip down my nose again, Mention that I hate it for making the laborer feel terrible. I really do. My new sunglasses have unfortunately proven themselves to be too large for my face and I am forced to push them up repeatedly. You love something quickly and quickly it fails you. I look around the orange streets. In a fantastic pair of sunglasses, I find I don't give a damn about anything. But when we return to our rooms I find I am very ill. I find I am feverish and tired. I find the need for bed to be the most overwhelming drug and I cannot get to bed quickly enough.

In the bedroom I once shared with Edmund I lie down to stare at my beloved ceiling. And I don't get up for a very long time. I don't know why he left; I don't know that I care. I just know I like to lie in bed. Sometimes the boy and I look at the photo of Edmund playing soccer, a document where he remains full of life, full of motion and aspiration. What we have here, I tell the boy on many days when we laze together looking at the photograph, Is evidence of failure, nothing more. Edmund's brother agrees. How agreeable he is these days when I stay so often in the back bedroom. Sometimes we take our dinners in bed, sausages from the butcher, smoked or precooked, or sometimes I allow Edmund's brother to cook as I shout instructions from bed. I love my bed. The assault of images and smells, the textures of the world outside my bed is such a siege. Yes it is a siege, the world outside my room. There are days, a few days when I go outside, but the weather brings me back. I cannot recall if it is the heat or the cold that makes me hurry back, it is everything. You see what happens when you become attached to things, I tell the boy, Now you see why I have always instructed you to resist being moved. Lucky for me I don't feel a thing, I say. Once I worked in a bank and read fat novels while I drank hot liquids. How I loved those novels and the lovers in them. You have no idea how well loved a woman in a novel is, I tell Edmund's brother. You read these novels early in your life and you come to believe this sort of adoration is possible, I say. Then one day you find out the truth, that these women

our novelists described were never women at all but men in
fact. The authors loved men; because of the times, they pre-
tended to love women. I light another cigarette. I am sure you
take my point, I say, How even in fiction love is impossible. The
boy says nothing. I sleep, I review my life and the events that
brought me to that back bedroom in the piazza with a strange
boy who spends hours building cities on the carpet. Sometimes
I let him bring me the chessboard, but I cannot bear to think
more than two steps ahead, the future feels invasive and I forget to castle my king. I ask him to read from the encyclopedia
descriptions for T.B. and jungle flu. Nothing seems a match.
When I feel well enough, I wrap myself in a blanket, sit in a
chair and watch the boy build block palaces. Behind our walls
the city seethes, full of sharp things to stab the retina. So safely
plain inside, so nicely nothing. They will have you believe in
description, that the apprehension of jangled views and rushing
sounds are the things that make up a life, but it is equally in-
spiring to take refuge in some dark corner of the brain, to tunnel in and avoid the manmade clamor others like to yell about.
Was there some sign I did not read, some warning Edmund
would leave? I go over it again and again, those Swiss nights.
That parrot in the rafters, did it live or breathe? Was it an effigy,
wired there to frighten a creature more frightening than a parrot, a squirrel perhaps or some sort of fruit bat? My traveling
companion sat upstairs with the windows closed, watching the
small white balls on the bedwear sweat for nearly two days

before coming down to forage for some cocoa and a hard roll. Melville will remain lost to me forever. Here we are, I tell the brother, waving my cigarette, Here we are. In Rome. Of all places. I speak in very short sentences like this. In song titles. It is a condition. Of my convalescence. I suffer, I tell the boy, From a mysterious illness. It may pass soon, I murmur. I'm certain that my health will soon improve, I repeat. Although another prognosis suggests I may never recover. I might not die, I tell the boy bravely, But I may have losses: memory, or the feeling in one leg. There is no way of telling and I will depend on you to be brave in the face of my misfortune. The brother builds his cities taller and taller as I tell him what to expect should I lose my mental faculties or the use of my hearing.

Several weeks have passed since Edmund's departure. I begin to take a detached interest in my own suffering. Suffering is useful for writing poetry, I tell the boy, though in truth writing poetry sounds exhausting. Perhaps anecdotal pleasure, I quickly amend. Except that you hate anecdotes, the boy tells me, adding a block to his tower, Or so you always say. That's true. I smoke thoughtfully. Yes, I finally say and leave it elliptical as a poet would. The trees outside shimmer and hurt so I take to wearing my dark glasses inside. Our rooms turn amber. I could be a beetle preserved, waiting patiently for my moment in posterity's sun. Your brother might be dead, I tell the boy, to hear myself say it aloud, because I like to feel worse when I feel awful. There is no telling what has happened to him since we last saw that marzipan moon of his face, I say. It is with great pleasure that I am miserable, blowing smoke out of the window, watching it drift into the piazza, the man across from us feeding pigeons, the boy by me with his cities. Gradually the idea of Edmund fades, he loses definition, becomes difficult to remember. Did he wear glasses? How exactly did his jaw go? Tomorrow, I tell the boy, Tomorrow we will continue your education, though there is plenty to be learned doing exactly what you are doing. I have no idea what the boy is doing but it is so pleasant here inside, miserable and the sun seems so glaring out there, even through my dark glasses. Does the world have to be so bright. Tomorrow, I tell Edmund's brother, Tomorrow we will attend to a different part of your education, one which has not been served by your efforts there on the carpet. A historical site perhaps or an exhibition, though the money is disappearing fast. Perhaps before we are thrown on the street we will go to an exhibition of some kind to improve our minds, I tell the boy. This is the sort of thing intellectuals do; spend their last farthings improving their minds. Of course then they starve to death in the gutter but we shall not let this deter us from our education. In truth, learning seems little compensation for death, at least such a humble one. If learning meant dying in a great explosion with my name and photograph printed in the newspaper, then it might be worth it. We will go tomorrow, I say, drawing the blanket around my shoulders as if tomorrow is a chilly wind from the north. But when tomorrow arrives, to-morrow finds me again by the window talking about tomorrow.

One morning I throw open the windows and breathe deeply. Today is the day I will venture out. God help me, if it kills me I will have some fresh air. After several enthusiastic breaths I run a bath, and pull my blue dress over my head. I buckle my shoes, take off my sunglasses and regard myself care-fully in the mirror. After a month or so indoors, the reflection is not too terrible if I glance quickly and avoid entirely the area around my eyes. In fact if I squint, I look pretty terrific. And if I only regard my legs then I am quite happy to leave our rooms. My legs have always been shapely, I tell Edmund's brother who has trotted in trailing a long woolen scarf. How it infuriates the glove buyers of this city that legs like mine cannot be purchased, I say. The boy is pulling over a chair, clambering up on it with the scarf, now trying to wind the woolen snake around my neck, choking me with the damn thing. Just a minute, I tell the boy before he winds the scarf up to my eyeballs. Just a damn minute. The boy jumps down from his chair, folds his arms and stares at me. He folds his arms! Now listen to me, I say sharpish, I am the adult so if there is to be any folding of arms around here, it will be mine that get folded. You are the child, I say. I am in charge. But as I say *I am in charge,* I suddenly feel very weak and want a sandwich. I suddenly want very much to watch the boy cut bread into fat slanting slices using a knife as long as his arm. I want Edmund's brother to butter it for me with the industrious focus he brings to such matters. I want to watch him repair where the cold butter tears the bread and being unable to fix it, to plaster the rips with slices of meat, pressing down so firmly he dents the bread. I look down at my shoes for comfort; they are always joined to the earth in a singularly comforting fashion. Why won't the brother make me a sandwich? I suddenly want one very much, yet I cannot ask. He is the child and I am the adult, not the other way around. Can't he see I need sustenance before we set out on our day of learning, our first in weeks or even months. The boy is in the kitchen. I can hear him replacing the cover on the little butter coffin. Are you having a sandwich? I call out, Are you eating, because we should leave, we have things to learn after so much time lolling around, we really have no time for lunch. A pause. I come to stand in the kitchen doorway. The hand holding the butter dish is halfway to the refrigerator. You can almost see the boy's brain throb as he calibrates what I am saying versus what I mean. It is our first lesson after a long respite, a lesson in the art of subtext. The boy turns, oh angel of confusion, you white-haired rapscallion, strafed by the light of the refrigerator like a little Titian angel. The lesson takes. With a sigh Edmund's brother replaces the butter on the counter and begins to unwrap the bread. With prosciutto! I shout, scampering to the living room window then back to the kitchen doorway, With prosciutto and maybe some mustard as well, only not too much. Patiently, the boy begins to saw the bread; I run back into the front room, no I skip, I swear to you after these weeks in bed, I skip, it is suddenly such an unbelievable joy, that the brother is making me a sandwich! That we afford bread! My shoes glitter in the morning light as I skip. Not too much butter, I call out, You are not spackling holes in the wall! I suddenly feel as if I am in a book where the heroine wants *life,* the author wants to fix it on the page, they both want to acknowledge *life,* to stop it from being so ephemeral for one goddamned second, to marvel at life in its meaningful minutiae. Yes, I am exactly like that with the brother making me a sandwich in the kitchen, *life*! All the dusty corners sparkle and the man across the way, perhaps he simply feeds the pigeons and isn't luring them inside one by one to feast on them, but if he does eat them, well isn't that also *life,* in its infinite riches, in the moments, the ticking, in the end of an illness, in the meat sandwich, in the eaten pigeon.

The boy's sandwich is quite the best I have ever tasted. I have no qualms about eating in the street, so I chew with gusto as we make our way through the city. We pass the Basilica San Clemente as I finish licking my fingers. I hold up my hand, showing Edmund's brother my greasy fingers. You see how much butter you used, so much that I am forced to lick my fingers clean? The objective, I remind the brother as I wipe my fingers dry, *Any* sandwich's objective is that the eater finishes her sandwich cleanly. Your sandwich eater should not be obliged to take personal hygiene into the streets of Rome. If

she does you have failed. Write this down in your green notebook, I tell him. Write that hygiene might be a variable consideration to *some* people, I say, knowing the boy will understand
exactly whom I speak of, But to the likes of us it is a number-
one priority. Certainly we would love to roam the city like wild
things with rank hair, we would love to be as bestial as our fore-
fathers, but times have changed, and we must change with
them. Some may demonstrate a *wild* streak by foregoing washing altogether; you and I know that the caprices of the brain are
not dependent on halfhearted grooming. Are we wealthy people? We are not, I tell the boy, Yet the clothes we own are as
kempt and clean as those belonging to the oppressive classes.
We sit on a bench to drink our water and gaze at the San
Clemente. I lean forward in a confessional manner, moved by
the ecclesiastic setting perhaps. Deep inside me I long to drop
on all fours and prowl the streets like a jackal, I whisper, I want
to bang into people, bite them, taste blood. The boy whimpers,
turning his head to look behind him. I would have matted fur
thronged with burrs, thorns in my hide, blistered gums and I
would be scarred and destroyed and flayed and never be still.
Yes. I lean back, slugging water. Yes, I would, I would not stop
to cook a meal. The water slides back into my throat. And yet I
do none of these things, I tell the boy, turning to him. These are
things we learn as the calendar pages turn. We may feel feral on
the inside, but we keep our clothes pressed, I tell him. This is
the contract we have with the world. I pass the bottle of water

to the boy. He flinches when our hands touch. His eyes are wide and staring, a thin film of perspiration coats his skin. His breath comes as if he has been running for miles. I cough; my silly monologue has upset him. Come now, I say with a nudge. Must we be so serious? He shakes his head quickly as if I might eat him if he disagrees. Above all we must never be too serious, I say, smiling. Unfortunately when I make the effort to smile as opposed to smiling naturally, it can be a fearsome sight. You know, I say, giving up the effort, It is beyond impossible to avoid traumatizing you. You will just have to accept it, I tell him. Accept the trauma now and deal with it later, or never, if you prefer. Together we gaze up at the cathedral. I stick a piece of grass in the side of my mouth only it is not a piece of grass at all. So I have to spit. I have to sit in front of the church spitting. Of course my old husband was a great fan of the church, I tell Edmund's brother when I am fully recovered. I will always remember him down on one knee praying for my eternal salvation, or something, I say, I could never hear his words exactly. Perhaps he was damning me. I take out my cigarettes, pressing a fist to my chest as I thump out a racking cough. Yes, it strikes me now that my old husband, down on his knees and crossing his shoulders, was in fact sending slanting looks back to where I stood with my books and papers. Every evening as I gathered up my studies to make room for our evening meal, my husband cursed me. Because there was a short time, after I left the bank and before I left my husband, when I believed things to be worthy of study and I ventured to study them, I tell the boy as he lights my cigarette. But in the end I stopped. I stopped when I found I was only ever something my husband imagined, I tell the boy. I am not entirely certain what this means but in looking at the church, I am moved to say it. Does this interest you at all? I ask the boy, outlining the church with my cigarette, crossing it in effect. I like the dome, he says. Aside from the dome, it seems like a fat lot of nothing to me, I say, Old men in dresses, skin like paper, muttering in Latin, all that history of nothing.

I stand up to inspect the church by a different angle. If we believed in God it would mean believing in many things, I say. There's a box I'd rather not open. The boy is still staring at the dome. This building was constructed hundreds of years ago; they had a thing called belief back then, I say, A little thing called faith. In those days. Good grief, why does the world move so slowly. Nothing moves quickly enough. I'm not saying this; I'm thinking it. A woman wearing a large brimmed hat walks in front of me to take some snapshots. Her hat is black with slender grey stripes at the very outer edge of the brim. I turn to find the boy staring at me, his eyes burning into my skull. What? I ask, startled by the intensity of his gaze. No hat! he says loudly. I was just looking, I say, but in fact I cannot seem to let go of my desire for a hat. Yet there is no money for a hat. If I express my desire for this thing, this hat, I am certain to be met with resistance. It is very clear that if I am interested in any sort of philosophical discussion about death and hats I will be met with arguments for prosciutto and cheese. I drop my cigarette, crushing it under my shoe. I stare up at the church as if it is a building I admire very much. I fold my arms and telescope my gaze professionally. I nod my head approvingly in case the boy is watching. Then I turn. In fact the boy is lying fully stretched on the bench behind me, eyes shut. My pantomime has been a waste. The woman, her hat, have disappeared. But not from my mind, not from my intention. The boy does not move, nor does he open his eyes. You do not need a hat, he says slowly. Wretch! I drop to my knees to murmur in his ear. I had a cat like you once, I say, She had a hard heart just like yours, like petrified wood. Edmund's brother opens his eyes and yawns. I get to my feet, a volley of shots resounds from the direction of my knees. Perhaps I would not be such a hard woman had I a hat, I say, Has that ever occurred to you? The sum total of my life boils down to this hatless state, this unloved and disrespected place. Edmund's brother sits up on the bench, his eyes glued to something behind my back. I spin around, shading my eyes from the sun's glare.

Across the piazza, a teacher in a flat black hat leads a snake of schoolchildren in front of the church. I do not care for the hat of this *professore,* it resembles a plate. You would never find me wearing a platter on my head, I say, turning back. Edmund's brother is sitting upright staring raptly, not at the hat, but at the children. Costumes, he murmurs. I join him on the bench.

The schoolchildren form two long rows of two. They all wear identical dreary caps, even the girls, and grey blazers with a crest stitched to the pocket. Uniforms, I say, Those are uniforms, not costumes. Satanically ugly uniforms, but uniforms all the same. Edmund's brother ignores me, he watches the children follow their teacher across the piazza until they disappear around the corner. Then he slumps down on the bench. I look from the boy to the spot where we last saw the schoolchildren, then back to the boy. Edmund's brother meanwhile stares at his fingernails as he does when he feels particularly depressed.

I take it that you would like a little grey blazer like your chums over there? His eyes flick up at me, then back to his fingernails. You have learned some life lessons these past weeks, I say. I can promise that not one of those grey-jacketed little pigeons knows a thing about life lessons. Some day out in life you will find yourself face to face with one of those princes and you will bash in his head. Educationally speaking, of course. I never condone violence, at least not initiating it. Does he understand me? The boy nods his head but as I am on the point of walking away, to secure something for our evening meal, he says suddenly, I don't know anything important. I stop, turn and regard him seriously. He looks away. I return to the bench.

Now, who do you think is really having a time of it, those poor little ones forced to march in rows like soldiers? He sighs. I take out a cigarette and tap it on the bench. There is nothing you could learn in school that I cannot teach you here outside in the nice weather, I say. You have questions; ask me a question. I light the cigarette and inhale deeply. Go ahead, I say, Fire away, what is it you wish to know? Immediately the boy gets up, turns around and sits back on the bench arranging himself differently. Okay, he says, What about— But my hand has flown up to shush him. Across the piazza, a woman has come out of the Basilica San Clemente. She wears a blue dress and a pair of white gloves and though she has a great mane of red hair there is no mistaking the spitting image of my aunt. My aunt had very short hair that she liked to cut herself and favored men's trousers chopped at the knee yet the similarity is undeniable. Here we are, the boy and I on our bench in Rome seventeen years after the death of my aunt and yet across the piazza is her exact double. The woman does not pause or glance in our direction. I remain transfixed until she moves out of sight.

Well, I say, leaning back, I can scarcely believe how that woman resembles my aunt. I stand up. I want to put my hands in my pockets as my aunt always did but I have no pockets. I cross my arms, as I believe my aunt would have done had she found herself without pockets. My aunt was so proud of my history prize, I tell Edmund's brother. When I went to visit my aunt on her deathbed, her nurses grouped around me to say how often she spoke of the grand things I was destined to accomplish. At the time I was full of myself as the young so frequently are, I say, I too thought my life would follow the glittering path forecast by my history prize. Alas this was not the case. But there is no excuse for the way I treated my aunt; if I could roll back time to treat her differently I would in an instant. Instead, I tell the boy, Instead I am forced to live with the image of myself smoking on her hospital bed as she drew her final breaths. You see, I had no idea what the word emphysema meant. At the time I believed emphysema inflamed the joints, similar to gout. I don't know who dispensed that information, I say, Perhaps I learned it at school. If I could do it all over, I tell the boy meaningfully, I would be thankful for the things for which I never showed thanks. Regret, I tell Edmund's brother, This is what we call regret. I think you know what I am saying, I say, I think you get my meaning. I look across the piazza at the space between buildings through which the woman disappeared. I wonder now if I might have loved my aunt, I say, If it is in fact love that brings on the pitching sensation I have when I see that woman walking out of the Basilica San Clemente. I would hate to think my efforts to resist love have all been in vain, I tell the boy thoughtfully, I hate to think I instruct you in a science I cannot myself master, but we must prepare ourselves that this may be the case. I had parents, of course, I say. Because we all have parents, even you, though they are heaven knows where. My parents never believed I had this quality, *potential.* They wanted a daughter, or more correctly a son, who followed the rules set out in Sally's little book. Of course had they possessed a son, he would not have owned such a book, oh no, he would have been given rocks to throw and sticks to shake. I grind out the cigarette. I wonder what my aunt would have done had some Toby called her a hard woman. I wonder if my aunt would have cared in the slightest. I doubt it very much for my aunt was an expert at never caring what anyone thought. Yes, I murmur, She was astonishingly good at that. Of course it is impossible to think that anyone called my aunt hard for she was revered wherever she went. When I was a girl we would often walk to town together and my aunt was treated like a queen in every shop we entered, so it is impossible that anyone would ever think to call her hard. Even horses liked my aunt; she once considered a career in horse training. Anyone in the town with a wayward horse knew to bring it to my aunt. In the end though my aunt could never answer to someone else, no, she wanted to never wake up at the same time and never walk the same path twice, I say. Perhaps she wasn't as celebrated as she might have been had she followed her father's dream and become a champion trainer of horses but my aunt danced to her own drummer.

I stretch back over the bench and look at the sky. I have an inordinately flexible back; it is quite possible for me to simultaneously keep both hands and both feet on the floor while simulating a bridge, though I have not done so in a long while. Two clouds above are stretched as long and thin as pencils. On her deathbed my aunt told me she had made a pledge to herself that she would wake at a different hour every day and every day taste something she had never tasted before. This is what we call a personal philosophy, I tell Edmund's brother, These sorts of pledges. And I guarantee you those pigeons in their hateful blazers know nothing about personal philosophies as they disgorge the right facts at the right time. My aunt could never take a job training horses, I say, Though that was her gift. She wanted to see every part of the globe. As difficult as it might be to believe, the truth is that my aunt could do anything she put her mind to; she just had to put her mind to it first. I look over at the boy. Most days I feel ashamed I am not the person my aunt thought I would become. I wish I could do something for her even though she is now deep in the ground having suffered a gruesome death from her lungs disintegrating. Mercy, I say, lighting another cigarette. We, the living, we think of the dead all the time when we fail them, when we do not rise to their expectations. I hold up the match and watch the flame burn closer and closer to my fingers. I wish I could do something in honor of my aunt, I say, shaking the match to extinguish it. I wish my aunt could look down on me now and think my life has not been wasted after all.

I look over at Edmund's brother. He has been sitting for some time now with his arms folded looking off into the distance with a tranquil expression. He does not look at me. Are you thinking what it might be like to die? I ask. He shakes his head. Because we have no idea, I say; Dying might very well be a pleasant sensation akin to a hot bath. We have no idea what death feels like but we know it looks like a tunnel. Yes, a tunnel with a pinpoint of light at the end. One after the other, we take our place in the ground. The boy continues to stare straight ahead of him. After a moment he turns to me, sucking in a larger breath than normal. He appears to be gathering his courage or something is stuck in his windpipe perhaps. I . . . I. He hesitates. Yes? I say.

I want to go to school, he says finally, dropping his head.

I blink several times in rapid succession. I feel as if I have been punched. I look at the church. I suck deeply on my cigarette. Well, I feel like I've been punched, I say, Punched in the stomach or, more accurately, the throat. The boy shrugs. It is as my mother said once when I was thirteen. A child will kill you over and over. I fold over, dropping my head to encourage some blood flow. As a child I fainted many times. Any test of physical exertion immediately found me flat on the floor with my toes pointing up. So I know what needs to be done at a time like this. After a minute I sit upright. Am I not providing you with the very best in education? I ask the boy, puzzled. He kicks at the ground. There's nothing there, I point out, You are not kicking anything unless I'm losing my eyesight. He stops kicking. I want a costume, he says, It's not fair. The boy is driving me insane, slowly, deliberately; I might as well have married him. You're talking about the uniform? I ask. You want a uniform? He nods. Clouds move across the sun. Come on, I say, Let's go home, I've lost interest in this day. Dutifully he gets up and follows, head bowed.

For the life of me, I say as we take an alley shortcut, I cannot understand your passion for school. You want to trudge around in two lines of two all day? The boy shrugs. He looks so miserable. I put my hand on his shoulder. I tell him how when we get home I will make him the biggest pancake he has ever seen. He will have difficulty finishing it off by himself, that's how big. Only two weeks earlier the mention of a giant pancake would have had the boy beside himself with delight. In fact even a week ago the boy spoke of that dinner with a rheumy nostalgia confined to pensioners. But when we arrive back in our rooms Edmund's brother remains morose, even as I am mixing batter for his pancake. He sulks silently while we eat. And afterward he stares gloomily into the dark courtyard while I try to tune the radio to the station he likes best. The radio makes a crackling sound and abruptly dies. Even then the boy does not turn from the window where he continues to stare out, kneeling on a yellow chair.

When Edmund stole away in the middle of the night he left behind a suit jacket in olive green. I take it from the wardrobe. Every boy should have a blazer, I say, Or a *costume* if you like. The boy glances at me over his shoulder. I hold up Edmund's coat in one hand, a pair of shears in the other. The boy's eyes widen and his mouth forms a perfect O. He climbs down from the chair, walking toward me with one hand toward the coat. *Blazer*, he says. That's right, I say, Come on, now. I help him into the coat. It reaches his knees. I hold up the shears. Ready? I ask. He closes his eyes and nods. As I hack at

the sleeves of Edmund's coat, I tell the boy, You see how there
is no reason to become depressed at every little thing? If you
wanted a uniform, you see how you might have turned to me
and requested one nicely instead of stomping across Farnese
like a depressive? The boy nods, turning so I can attack the
back of the coat. I made curtains for my husband once, I tell
the boy, clipping the strings that hang like a fringe from the
bottom of Edmund's chopped coat. My husband was a first-
rate sleeper as long as the room was pitch dark, but the most
trivial sliver of light was enough to keep him tossing and turning until dawn. Once it was dawn, well he found it impossible
to sleep if the sun was even *thinking* about rising. One night, as
the moonlight shone into our bedroom and my husband fret-
ted and became feverish, I offered to make curtains. If there
was one thing that old schoolmistress taught until we were
blue in the face it was the different techniques of needlework.
But just because you are hammered with some technique over
and over until the constrictions of the teaching tighten around
your throat, it does not mean you excel at the thing. At least
this has been the case in my experience. I tried to oblige my
husband's need for curtains, I was still fresh from my days at
the bank and thought of nothing but my husband's wishes day
and night, but I found I could not. I found the more effort I
made to assemble a pair of curtains the more terrible those
curtains became; they were dingy with the sweat of my labor,

lopsided and uneven. Worst of all, I had chosen lace for the fabric. As you might guess, lace is not the wisest choice for banishing daylight. I step back from the boy to assess the blazer. The difficulty is the shoulders. In the waist and in the arms, Edmund's jacket now fits his brother very well. I will need to hem the waist and arms of the coat but nothing can be done about the shoulders; they hang over the boy's actual shoulders by several inches. If anyone asked me, I tell him, I would say that is some fantastic uniform. I help him out of the coat, thread a needle and begin to hem. You can imagine what my husband thought when he saw my efforts, I continue. He chose me because he thought I was the best of the bank tellers; suddenly it seemed I was not the best at all, but quite possibly the worst. Picture his despair. One thing is certain; my husband immediately deduced his terrible mistake. Well it was not so long afterward that I found myself sitting by the pool making the colored lights swing, regarding the rats in the pool, questioning the love of my cat. The curtains were hung in the parlor where no one ever slept. Some girl from town was hired to craft dark panels for our bedroom where I am certain they hang to this day. I tie a knot in the thread and break it off with my teeth. Here, I say, handing Edmund's brother the altered blazer, Try this on. With an eagerness I have not seen in weeks, the boy pulls on the coat and gallops to the mirror. The boy's little jacket is not a replica of the blazers he admired on the

schoolchildren at the Basilica San Clemente, but it has the ear-
marks of a uniform. With an enormous smile, he turns, looking
at the front, assessing the back, flicking away bits of lint. Yes, I
murmur, standing behind him, I like it very much. Once more
he turns but instead of facing the mirror, the boy throws his
arms around my waist and buries his head in my stomach. You
like it? I ask. He nods his head up and down vigorously, no
doubt taking the opportunity to wipe his nose.

I wake in the middle of the night, my arms wrapped around
the pillow. The room is very dark; I hold the clock an inch from
my eyes, still I cannot make out the time. I remember how he
smelled lying next to me here on the pillow and how, suspended
over me, he blocked out the light. Apparently he left because
he found me *hard*. And yet Edmund hated words like *hard*.
Edmund never used a short word if he could find one containing
a few more letters or another syllable. Edmund would have used
a word like *durable* or even *implacable* before it crossed his mind
to use a word like *hard*. In fact there are a thousand words
Edmund would have chosen before he used an ordinary word
like *hard*. If he were going to use a word like hard he would have
used it in an ironic way, in a way to suggest that the thing he described, in this circumstance me, was in fact the opposite of
hard. For Edmund not to have described me to Toby as *obdurate*
or *remorseless* must have meant he found me *soft*, or *delicate;* or in
the more likely words of Edmund, *compassionate* or *merciful*. My
one strength, at least my most obvious strength is to never

abandon a notion I first find unsettling. I may seem to forget, but I have stored the idea in my brain for further rumination. As soon as Toby told me that Edmund left us because he found me hard, a woman so hard she had never baked him a pie, something rattled me about the comment and I put it away to examine when I found the time.

The next morning I have hot milk waiting for the boy when he wakes up. Blue roses gather in the bowl's center and vines trail along the edge of the bowl; it is the boy's favorite. The bowl is also my favorite, but today I offer it to Edmund's brother. He has slept in his new blazer and the thing is a map of creases. Once Edmund disappeared, the boy stopped asking to be carried to his milk. So I am standing over him brandishing the milk like something I have won. He sits up in bed suspiciously, unnerved to see me up and dressed at such a premature hour. I set the bowl gently on the table next to him. I say nothing, preferring to wait, the better to build to my point. I walk to the door, walk to the window and clear my throat. When I can bear it no longer I go to the foot of his bed and observe him as he addresses the milk. After a minute the boy's eyes flick up to me. Today is an important day, I say, Can you guess why? He shakes his head, blowing on the milk to cool it. Get your green notebook, I say, This morning we are going to learn some new and wonderful things. Since you arrived in Rome, how many hours have we given over to physical pursuits? Edmund's brother shrugs. Exactly, I confirm, Zero, that's how many. Hey, the boy says. Are we going to play soccer? With slow deliberation I cross one arm under the other folding them into a pretzel. It maddens me to be interrupted, as the boy well knows. To turn back when I have set out on the journey of the idea, or in this case, when I have felt some anticipation for the day that lies ahead when on so many days I feel nothing more than irritation that a day contains its twenty-four hours instead of a more charitable fourteen; nothing is more painful to me. Hardly anything. *Noooo,* I say. We are not going to play soccer. Do I look like a soccer player to you? The boy sighs. There exist more thrilling pastimes than chasing a ball up and down a wretched park, I say. Like what? he asks. I struggle to cling to my original elation. Today we are going to bake a pie, I tell him. The boy frowns. You heard, I say, First we will bake it then we will present it to our ancient landlord down below. I make a little flourish with my hand and bow like a courtesan. In a few hours I might do the same to old Marcolini but with a pie in my hand. Really? The boy says doubtfully. He is making me insane. Why is it, I ask, sitting and slumping on the edge of the bed, That whenever I have an inspired idea you stomp all over it with your little foot? I could have a plane outside waiting to take us on safari yet I wager the corners of your mouth would pull down. *Africa?* You would say, *Aren't we going to play soccer?* Have you any idea how demoralizing it is to tell you my plans only to hear about soccer? I stand and walk away, intending to leave the room. But when I reach the door, I spin around. And why do you sound so surprised? I ask. Do you think I can't put my mind to a pie? The boy shrugs. He has picked up his bowl again and is taking a tentative sip of milk. I fold my arms and widen my eyes. My heart is racing. What do you have to say about it? I ask. Edmund's brother gazes up at the ceiling. You know, I say, Some little boys would be very, very interested in learning how to bake a pie. Some of those monsters would be up and running with their green notebooks, jotting down information, filing it away for another occasion. They would be *skipping* they were so transported, I say. Yet I have never seen you skip. Not once. Are you even a child at all? I ask. Edmund's brother sets down the bowl. I just don't think *baking* is a good idea, he says. I feel the day slipping from me already. Oh, don't you? I say. And why should I listen to you, a someone who thinks sleeping in a blazer goes by the title *good idea?* Are you the king of intelligence; is that it? Were you installed while I was in the kitchen heating your blessed milk? And your coronation, did that take place while I was bearing the hot milk down the corridor to you in my favorite bowl? The boy pulls back the bedcovers and bends down to pick up a pair of socks he then expends a great amount of effort trying to get onto his feet. You are not the king, I say and leave him with his socks to retreat to the back bedroom.

From a tin marked *Tea,* I count several bills out onto the bed. Exactly enough to buy ingredients for a nice pie. We will see who is a hard woman. I fold the notes and place them in my brassiere but immediately the notes feel like razors and I am forced to remove them.

Edmund's brother turns to me when I walk into the front room, his new little schoolboy blazer misbuttoned. Have you ever made a pie before? he asks. And they say a child will humanize a person. I take out a cigarette. I light it and stare at him. I hope you never marry, I say, waving away the smoke to see him better. She will need to be some saint this wife of yours in order to bear her life. I blow smoke out my nose, this would frighten a normal child; he would take me for a dragon and run screaming or bend his little head to my breast so I could comfort him with tender words, all the while feeling extremely important and very adult. Why don't we just buy some pastries? he asks, Some cornetti or cannoli? Those are good. I push past him to take my own coat from the cupboard. Because that would defeat the entire purpose. The entire purpose, I say, In case I failed to make it clear, is to bake a *pie*. Anything else makes no sense at all and we might just as well spend our day in some dusty museum pointing at fossils. Look, I say, in an effort to make peace, Sometimes I feel tired of life and when I feel tired of life I like to do something completely unexpected. Something unexpected even to myself, as if I am thinking another person's thoughts rather than my own. While Toby's hardwoman comment is ludicrous—and believe me, I have given it a decent amount of thought, as one must when such a comment is leveled—Toby is correct when he says I never baked Edmund a pie. Now it is quite possible that we will never see your brother again, and when we are assured of that, we will make the proper arrangements. In the meantime, why should I not bake a pie? Why should we not challenge our abilities? Are we above such things? For heavens sakes, are we *afraid?*

I don't think I am boasting when I say that in leaving our rooms the boy has seen my point and recognized it as the superior one. Though he is still churlish. Your blazer is incorrectly buttoned, I inform him as I pull the gate closed. I wait for him to remedy his error then give him my hand to cross the street. Edmund's brother, at seven, might be of the age to not need a hand to cross the street, certainly he has crossed the street on his own on the occasions I find it unbearable to leave the house, still there are times when I feel benevolent and need to extend a hand and at those times the boy is quite right to take it. We cross the Minerva and bear toward Cestari. I am filled with hope today, full of the promise that a new project brings. I dare not mention it to Edmund's brother since he will want to hurl such a day to the ground and murder it with his shrunken foot. My urge is to grin from ear to ear because Toby is such a fool, but I force my grin into a grimace, as if I am not quite sure where the grocer lies and must summon all reserves of intelligence, including my mouth, to locate it.

They used to bind the feet of women in China, I tell the boy as we wait for the streetlight to change in our favor. Perhaps they still do, how would we know for certain? Anxious to get on, I press the button that accommodates pedestrians. You've already pressed that, the boy says, You won't make the light change any quicker by pressing it again. I take out a cigarette and treat myself to a sigh. I am smoking a thousand cigarettes today. My god what a headache you are, I say, digging in my bag for matches. I can scarcely believe the pricks and jabs I sustained last night sewing you a little blazer, only to have you no happier today than you were yesternoon. I locate matches and light the cigarette, marching across the street on our green. If your happiness is only good for a few hours, it's scarcely worth the effort. I'm finding a certain attraction to this word scarcely and want to continue using it as often as possible. What the devil is wrong with you? I ask the boy smokily. The boy hunches up his shoulders, shrugging. He is behaving oddly. I exhale, looking down at him out of the corner of my eye. Certainly he *appears* the same. And then, as I turn, I see the shoes.

Stop! I shout, coughing. Edmund's brother, speeding on, is forced to turn back, which he does lazily, sauntering back with his hands in his pockets. What *now?* he says rebelliously. Unable to speak, I jab my finger at the shop window. Religiously, we stare at them. You must have these, I whisper. Your new blazer deserves these sandals. The shoes are golden brown with a triangular pattern carved into the toe area. Mine, he says quietly. Yes, I murmur, stomping on my cigarette, Yes they are.

A tedious encounter with a shoe salesman follows this sweet moment. The relevant points are these: the shop has one remaining pair in the boy's size; the left sandal happens to have a tear in its strap; the horrible salesman happens to have disappeared into the lavatory for a moment while the boy and I were shopping. Why does it matter how the strap became torn. We gain our discount, laying our money on the countertop so as not to touch the horrible man's hand, and continue on our way.

We will fill our pie with apples, I say happily, So that Mr. Marcolini recognizes our gift is not simply some sweet frivolity but in fact a symbol of union between our nations. I have never baked a pie, I tell the boy, For the simple reason that I despise any art that cannot contain improvisation. Neither do I know the proper calisthenics for pie-making, as I have never seen one being baked, I continue, Though I have certainly smelled them. The filling is simple, cut apples, sprinkled sugar, but I know from my time in the kitchen that flour and water together make glue. And so we must be careful. In baking, proportions are all, I tell the boy. We will need numbers, ratios. I stop speaking. Edmund's brother is scrutinizing his feet as we walk and his lips are moving faintly. Are you talking to your shoes? I ask. He looks up, self-consciously. No, he says weakly. Ah, I say, looking behind him. I am embarrassed sometimes by his little fantasies. I move my head slightly to behold something in the distant sky, a kite. Your green notebook? I ask quietly. The boy puts his hands into his blazer pockets, rummaging. We both know your notebook will not fit in there, I say. And we both know that the reason your notebook will not fit in your pocket is because I purchased the largest size available. Do you recall begging me to spend extra that you might have the largest notebook? He nods. Well done, I say, You have remembered one thing without writing it down, we will see how you manage with the rest of the day. Tonight you will go to your bedroom directly after supper and notate everything you have learned about pie-making in your green notebook. Fine, he says. Fine, I tell him. And you will do so without your sandals. They will remain in the kitchen with me. Fine, he says defiantly. And we continue on to the grocer's in silence.

When we reach the shop, I stop outside and light a cigarette. Here's the thing, I tell the boy. This is my first effort at a pie and I won't have it fail. If I fail in this pie, I tell him, It will be a blow to my ego the likes of which we have not seen. I have completed tasks of such inordinate difficulty that some small pie will not be overly challenging, I say, But I cannot assume that the exact ratios of butter and flour and water will spring to mind at the precise moment I need them. We assess each other, the brother and I. I fancy my look is as searching as his is vacant. They might know the numbers in the grocer's, the boy suggests. Speak up, I say while I consider his plan. But do we trust the Romans? I ask, pacing, Will they trick us because we do not belong in their country? Or in a bid to be helpful will they invent something they believe we want to hear? He looks at me, the boy, deep into my eyes and nods thoughtfully, not *yes, yes I agree* nods but more slow thinking nods. Edmund's brother is becoming a man. Only a month ago he would have pulled at the seat of his trousers and left me to make all our life decisions. Today he holds my gaze like a man, a short man in a boy's sandals, yet clearly a comrade in the deliberation of our journey together in life. Of course there will be moments when I cannot allow him to be that man, and they will arrive shortly, but at this moment there is some succor in having my gaze so boldly held.

We will go to one grocer; we will ask him for the numbers and the exact ingredients, I say firmly, Obviously we know flour, butter, sugar, salt, but might there be more things or fewer? Or even something wild and altogether unexpected, borage for example? We will listen closely to this grocer; then we will corroborate this information with numbers we gather from another grocer. We will compare the two and if the information differs we will go to a third grocer. This third grocer's numbers will undoubtedly agree with one of the two preceding grocers. A look of doubt passes over the boy's face. This is a brilliant plan, I say, arguing with his silence. He tilts his head. *What?* I ask. The urge I have to stamp my foot or pinch him once, hard, I place into words. What? I repeat, not unkindly. Well, I'm wondering, Edmund's brother says with slow care — how quickly he can take an admirable trait and make it irritating. Do they even have pies in Rome? I concede the boy has a point. Through the pastry shop windows, I have yet to see a pie in Rome.

Dear god. I lead the boy to a fountain and we sit on its side together to consider this new information. I have woken with a great deal of ambition; it will take more than pastries to defeat me this morning. Crossing the piazza, a mother stops to fuss at her son, wiping his mouth with her thumb. She glances at me sternly. I reach out and begin smoothing the boy's hair. Edmund's brother has extremely good hair; he will retain it well into his life. I have no idea what I am doing. He leans away from me, glaring. I try attending to his collar, taking it out of his sweater, tucking it back in, but I am being impeded by the shoes looped around his neck by the laces. The mother stares at us, one hand on her son's shoulder. She curls her lip as she takes in the botched hemming of the boy's blazer. Let's go, I snap, pulling the boy off the fountain. We need to make this damn pie before I lose my mind entirely.

As we cross Rome we take great pleasure in pitying the ridiculous boy and his undistinguished life; together we imagine his miserable rise to small-town clerk and paper-fetcher. And then, as we near the Fontana di Trevi, we have an inspired idea. Tourists.

Tourists will give us the pie numbers.

We arrive at the fountain as the last members of a tour group heave themselves aboard a bus. Wait! The boy shouts, running and waving his arms. But it is too late. The bus grinds into gear and disappears around the corner, leaving us among blowing papers and plastic cups, coughing from the exhaust, looking around in desperation. Spanish teenagers throw coins in the fountain; a Japanese businessman dandles his feet in the water. Edmund's brother indicates a woman taking a photograph. No, I say quietly, She is German, trust me. Defeated, we stare at the boy's new sandals. Yes, they are purchased; still they please us. We find them beautiful. And as much as I have schooled the boy to understand that beauty can never be bought, I'm afraid his sandals are beautiful and were bought and do in fact bring joy.

Look! The boy says suddenly, pointing, Latecomers. An elderly couple rushes across the piazza. When they realize the bus has left without them, their shoulders sag and they regard each other sorrowfully. Edmund's brother glances at me. Old people, I whisper. The boy takes hold of my pocket; I am in retreat, whimpering. They are so *aged*. He grips my pocket tightly with his little pincers. We never thought it was going to be easy, he says, boldly. I will speak to him about that later. I place my fingers against my eyebrows and push them into groomed hoops. There will be a time in my life when someone will do such things for me. There will be swimming pools without rats; I will eat food from a plate instead of digging for remainders in the sofa cushions. Now is not that time. But such thoughts make certain transitions bearable.

A shortcut behind the Colonna takes a good ten minutes off a trip to the river from the latecomer section of the city. When ill-treated by this or that class of citizens, a swift shortcut usually undoes the damage. *Knowing better* is implicit in the shortcut. Action, I tell the brother, Action always, words rarely. You see how there is no need to trumpet our superiority over these foul latecomers, I say, We simply take the shortcut. I follow the boy, clambering over a low wall, pinching our noses as we skirt a line of rubbish bins. I don't like what I saw back there, I tell the boy, unpinching my nose as we leave the alley. You allowed a latecomer to rile you; there is no lower class than a latecomer, we do not accept humiliation at their hands. If there is humiliation to be had we will choose when and where to accept it and it will never be at the hands of any latecomer. I lead him toward the river.

On the bridge, a slight breeze from the river shifts the dank city smell toward us. Together we inhale it and name it refreshing. If anything serves to intoxicate the brother and me, it is the thrill of knowing better. We lean on the bridge railing to watch the sun set. Don't you see, the latecomer is to be pitied, I tell the boy, Because the trait affects his entire life. I've seen it begin at birth, I tell him. I know latecomers who refuse to leave the womb. They sit and cook for more than ten months, refusing to appear at the suggested nine. And it just gets worse. As a child they cannot leave the bed, as an adolescent, school is one long dream. You want to believe that their inner lives are enthralling, that in here—I tap my head—there is rich sustenance for a dreamy life. Oh, I sigh elaborately and place a foot on the railing to regard my buckle shoe, If only this were the case. But

I swear to you a man named Herman Melville was never a late-comer, no not Shakespeare either. None of the greats in other words were ever *en retard,* I say so as not to rhyme. The boy is never one to shake a rhyme he likes. We look at the boy's new sandals and he smiles with the serenity of a cat on a ledge, not my cat, who was too fat to get up on any ledge, but an agile cat. How calm we are, given our setbacks. You know I used to think I was tired of adoration, I say, apropos of nothing, But these days I find I am not. These days I am bored by the latecomers of this rank city. The boy bends to his sandal. I have taught him well; he wipes a drop of river water from it. I am bored by those who will not share their knowledge, I say, Especially of something as innocent as the numbers for a pie. But then the hoarding of knowledge is always vexing, I add. I like to think I have encouraged you to be generous with what you know, I tell him, but I realize that in fact the opposite is true, I have always suggested the boy hold his tongue. However now is not the time for self-reflection. Those latecomers drinking their smug coffees know exactly how much flour a pie takes. They may not have humiliated us but they hoarded information and for that no punishment is too grim. If the police stopped flirting with the local tarts for ten minutes they would have that old couple in cufflinks right now. I say cufflinks but I mean handcuffs. It is perilous to stop me mid-tirade for corrections of vocabulary. There is a fossil, I announce, pointing wildly in the direction of our rooms, Languishing in a wide-armed chair on the Piazza

Navona, who has been denied pie. Somehow those responsible for it are free to roam our streets instead of sitting in the electric chair where they surely belong. My words mingle with the rotten river air. I am getting carried away; I appear to be recommending execution for withholding a recipe. But this day has meant to crucify me since its genesis. And it isn't just a recipe, I tell the boy defensively, All around me I am being prevented from reaching my potential. If I ever prevent you from reaching your potential you have my permission to bring it to my attention. Politely, I add. *Politely.* What kind of society is it where a woman cannot bake a pie if she so chooses? We've gone to hell, I tell the boy, We've gone to the bloody dogs. I don't know why I say bloody, it immediately strikes me as pretentious. Bloody sounds stuck-up and pretentious and vaguely military but I like the way it feels in my mouth and immediately vow to use it again as soon as possible. There are times when you can decide something is contrary to what you first think and make it so simply by force of will. If I decide bloody is an appropriate description of the situation, then it is not pretentious, it is accurate, no matter if I am neither well educated nor a member of the military. But since I would prefer not to hear Edmund's brother say bloody every thirty seconds, bloody is perhaps better left for the inside of my head. I take out a cigarette. The river is dismal. I am alone. Terribly alone. Resigned to a continual failing. Resigned to the looks. Alarm, a sniff, the sound of scraping chairs. I am a scourge, I say aloud. Edmund's brother takes no notice; I believe he is talking to his shoes again. *Scourge* lifts my spirits a bit. Scourge sounds epic and terrible. A scourge on your house. No, no, it is grandiose to think of myself as a scourge. I am invisible. But as I stare at the river I feel suddenly emboldened. I renounce your pie, I say quietly. Samina, wherever you are and I hope it is some religion's form of a fiery underworld. Perhaps I never baked a pie for Edmund and perhaps he left me for that reason, but he may well have left for other reasons. Has this mother of his ever read Melville? Has Samina? Fine, I never *finished* the whale book, but I would have, had I not left the book in the bloody Alps. I am a competent if impatient reader. Which is precisely why, *Samina,* if I had those numbers I could make the pie. Not just that pie; any pie. It does not take a genius to bake a pie if the numbers are provided. Of course I like to prove these things to myself, even if Samina now lies beneath the dock leaves in the ground. It is an imperative principle of humanness to prove things to yourself or you might just as well be dead. But this is not simply a matter of proof, to self or Samina. Old Marcolini could use a surprise, a nice surprise. The last was a hairy spider near his bidet one morning; we woke to his screams. But I have found this is the way with acts of charity. There is always an impediment. Yes, one after the other until you've lost the will for good entirely and wish the whole world would fall into the toilet. If the pie is not to happen today, or ever, it is no fault of mine. If the next time I see Marcolini I bite off his head instead of presenting something hot from the oven; who can blame me. I gave it my best effort. Some other day, I tell Edmund's brother, Some other time we will make the pie. And we both stare down at the new sandals.

Now that we have forgotten the salesman, how much pleasure the shoes give us. The leather is so firm, the buckles astonishing and bright. I knew as soon as I saw the sandals that the boy would enjoy shoes that buckle like mine. Unspeakable joy can be found in the buckling of a shoe. For one thing there is the daily consideration of which hole the buckle's prong should enter. This usually depends on the thickness of one's sock though it can also depend on other factors like water retention in the foot. Over time, because one type of stocking is often favored, the leather strap becomes marked with a thin line of darker brown. Sooner or later Edmund's brother will find no need to test one bucklehole over the other for the proper fit, he will know instantly, from this dark line, which hole the buckle likes best. How many delights lie in store for the boy. And if he can learn to keep about his body small joys to comfort him in the face of assaults, whether doled out by latecomers or glove buyers or shoe salesmen, he will never fail in his journey to become a great man.

The more I think about it, I tell him, The more I hate the idea of baking this pie, in fact the entire notion fills me with revulsion. I cannot begin to compare the smell of a satchel I once owned to the smell of a baking pie. I light a cigarette. It is simply beyond my ken, as the Scottish say, I murmur. The boy and I look deeply into the unnerving green of the river water. I think I would like to start a business, I say suddenly. If my aunt had survived the disease that took her so criminally young, she would have liked to see me in business. I hook my shoe into the railing that prevents the depressed from taking their lives without a struggle. What sort of business would you see me in? I ask Edmund's brother, handing him my cigarette. He takes a long thoughtful drag. A science shop? he says. We both observe a little dog by the bank of the river ferret at something in the ground. Interesting, I say, taking the cigarette back and inhaling deeply. That's very interesting, I repeat. What the devil is a science shop? The boy shrugs. I like science, he says. Do you now? I murmur. It certainly seems a noble venture, a science shop; a place where members of society interested in the sciences could enter to the ding of a little bell and set about purchasing items of various sorts. I turn to the boy. What sort of items do science shops sell? I ask. The dog has stopped digging and trots away holding a glove in its mouth. Microscopes? the boy offers, Goggles and telescopes, little dishes, poking sticks. I nod to stop him. Always advisable not to give the boy too much rope. Given enough rope he always hangs himself. There's a relief, I tell him, I thought you meant diseases and antidotes. Yes, I like this idea. I throw my cigarette into the river and we watch it float away.

The most appealing part of the science shop would be a

snug corner I would turn into a sitting area. I would place several large armchairs in a corner gathered around a table. On the
table I would set an enormous ashtray, then I would serve coffee and cakes made by some local girl who loved to bake. All the
leading minds would hunker down in the corner of the science
shop to discuss the leading theories of the day. Oh yes, I liked
this idea very much the more I considered it. It made me want
to use the word *leading* over and over again to signify the break-
ing edge of reason and theory, all the glittering interesting
things, the jewels of our modern times. The more I think of it,
the more I want it. How strange to be doubly good, I say. As
you know I was the big winner of the history prize at the school
I attended. Yet here I find I might also be some sort of Madame
Curie, I say, Only not a pioneer of course. I find it distasteful,
that sort of arrogance. The Science Shop, I say. I like it very
much. I can even see the sign, a wrought-iron affair with a symbol of some kind, something to signify learning and profundity.
Edmund's brother nods. And cake, he adds, Don't forget cake. I
look at him quickly to see if he is laughing, but the boy contem-
plates the water with a stern expression. I think perhaps no one
symbol can signify both higher science and cake, I say. He nods.
I see, he says softly. I fold my arms and stare into the clouds. A
pair of spectacles perhaps, I say. The boy shakes his head. People will think we sell glasses. He is correct of course. But the
more I think about it, the more difficult it becomes to find the
perfect symbol. A telescope is too limiting for the range of

services we will provide. It is a conundrum to be certain. The boy takes the packet of cigarettes from my hand, shakes one out and lights it. We will need a great deal of lire, he says. He knows this drives me mad. I grip the railing tightly to control my temper. Please don't say *lire,* I tell him quietly. You know how it upsets me when you use that word, please say money. He nods. And yes, I murmur, We will certainly need *money* in order to launch our enterprise. We both look up and down the river as if a treasure chest might suddenly float by. Toby? The boy says. I take the cigarette from him and inhale deeply. Yes, I say. Perhaps that brother of yours has sent some more bills. Despairingly, the brother looks at his shoes. I nudge him. Come now, a few coins spent on sandals will not prevent us from owning our Science Shop. I offer my hand, Let's go find that smelly friend of Edmund's.

We make our way toward Toby's slowly, discussing the various materials we will stock in our shop. I exalt the wonders of the idea corner; we agree we will serve coffee superior to any train station café. In truth we chatter nervously because neither the boy nor I has any desire to see Toby again. We would rather be forced to dance in public than to ever set eyes on that waiter again. How unfortunate, I tell the boy as we cross Farina, That you and I are forced to resemble beggars. Alas this is what your brother and his cohort have visited upon us. Toby has never forgiven us for drinking so much coffee that day, I tell Edmund's brother, An episode that was not entirely our fault, since it was Toby after all who brought us the coffee and it was his job to cut us off when he saw the negative effect of so much caffeine. For all Toby knew, we might have been suffering some sort of allergic reaction that morning. One more sip might have found us flat on our backs on the café tiles. Had that been the case, that we expired on his floor, Toby's grievous lack of perception would have put him out of a job entirely, I tell the boy. He should thank his lucky stars that you and I have such strong constitutions. You see what happens when cretins are hired for even the simplest of tasks? I ask, digging in my bag for my sunglasses. In the future, when Toby comes crawling to our Science Shop groveling for employment, I think he will regret the way he treated us, I tell Edmund's brother, Though of course we will be magnanimous. In the future, no matter how execrable he is or how wretched his manners, we will let Toby sweep the shop floor or wash the cake plates because he was once a friend of your brother's and this is how civilized people behave.

Toby rushes over as soon as we walk in. It is the evening hour and the café is full and smoky. A loud bassoon and drumming noise comes from one corner in the name of music. What are you doing here? Toby asks, leading us into shadows. Toby calls me by my second name; that is my family name, not my given name. I prefer to be called by my family name only by those who know me intimately. That name is for those with whom I have tangled. I do not wish to be vulgar, but I hate vagueness of any stripe. For everyone else, my first name is familiar enough, especially for those the boy and I consider rancid. I smooth my dress nicely. Behind Toby's back, the boy is gagging and pinching his nose, making a show of Toby's rancidity. He is being very funny. I pretend not to see him. Can't we have a drink, Toby? I ask, looking at him over the top of my sunglasses. Are we no longer citizens of this city? Has our free will been robbed by the *scugnizzi* while I was preoccupied? Toby glances around the café fearfully. Listen to me, he hisses urgently. I am beginning to enjoy myself. I suddenly feel very important and I haven't all day, on the contrary, I have felt small and insignificant on the day I planned to bake a pie and present it to our Mr. Marcolini. Now Toby is making me feel very important and I want it to last as long as possible. I need you to go away, he says, blocking me from an empty table and pointing at my sternum. Hm, I say, testing the quality of a nearby tablecloth, I wonder why are you making us feel so unwelcome. Toby stares at me with hatred. The last time we saw you it was no different, I remind him. The last time we saw you, we were both insulted, both the boy and I. Both of us, I say one more time. You called me a hard woman, I remind Toby. A pause. Toby says nothing. Or was it dark? I ask, leaning forward. Back in our rooms I was unsure whether I misheard you, did you perhaps say dark, not hard? Or perhaps you said hard woman when you meant dark woman? Toby makes a strange noise from his throat. I really don't have time for this, he says, drawing out a white envelope. Here, he holds it out to me, This came from

Edmund. I snatch the envelope. Edmund who? I say and we race from the café, beeping loudly, snatching pastries from a passing waiter, waving them at rancid Toby as we go.

We might not go back there, I tell the boy as we rush down the street. I might not have the patience for Toby's promiscuous approach to hygiene, I say, And the casual way he inflicts insults. As if I care what Toby thinks I am. He's rancid, the boy agrees, shoving the last of a pastry in his mouth. I hold up Edmund's envelope, pinching it between my thumb and forefinger. Look at this, I say, There can't possibly be any cash in here. There goes our dream, smashed at our feet like ... I cannot think what our smashed dream is like, I say. Plates? the boy suggests. Yes, I say, A big pile of smashed plates. I inspect Edmund's envelope. Well, I say, It appears that the great men of science will have to find another haven, for your brother has deemed their needs irrelevant. For three weeks or months or whatever I have been ill, I tell Edmund's brother, And though I have tried to protect you from the truth, I need to tell you now, for the sake of honesty, that I have suffered. I drum the boy on the head with a corner of the sealed envelope. For three weeks I suffer, now Edmund sends some letter as if I have not suffered? How dare he? I ask, genuinely perplexed. I stare at the boy and he at me. He opens his mouth; quickly I widen my eyes; it is our special signal, *consider what you are about to say.* The boy thinks, then he opens his mouth even farther. I widen my eyes as much as I can, wider than I ever have. Then my eyes begin to hurt so

I stop. Maybe Edmund sent us a check, he says. I look at him suspiciously, my eyes now their normal size again. I look at the boy, then at the envelope. And what if it does contain a check? I ask. What does that make us, his whores? I make as if to throw Edmund's envelope in the gutter but I keep hold of it. We should be kept by him, but remain unseen—is that the idea? I ask as we continue on our way. Does the man have no conscience?

When we arrive at our rooms I do not rush into the kitchen to greedily attack the envelope with a knife. Put on your pyjamas, I tell the boy when we arrive. The boy does not own pyjamas, but my intent is clear. Sleepwear, I call after him as he scampers down the corridor. I place Edmund's letter on the kitchen table. I pour two glasses of water, wind my hair tightly on top of my head and light a cigarette. I think more clearly with my hair up. My temples are tighter, some beneficial chemistry happens there in the brain. I pace back and forth, sucking on the cigarette, looking over at the envelope as if it sits in a pool of bright light and I am in charge of its torture. The brother runs in, wearing soft bedthings and smelling very good. We sit on the yellow chairs provided by Edmund's father, taking a moment to establish our comfort by scooting the chairs forward and back and from side to side. Following my lead, the boy takes a few swallows of water. Finally I reach out and tear open the envelope. No check, I report, drawing out a thin sheet of paper. I lay it carefully on the table and we both stare at it while I smoke. You know I find myself strangely attached to our idea of a science shop, I tell the boy. Though we only began to conjure a dream of our business this afternoon, I have become so invested in this idea that I find the lack of a check morbidly depressing. I inhale deeply. How shall I get over it? I ask. The boy pushes Edmund's letter toward me. Maybe Edmund says something good, he says. Maybe we should read it. I look at the letter lying on the table, pallid as skin. And I shiver. You read it, I say, tapping it. Let's challenge your reading skills, hm? The boy picks up Edmund's letter and begins reading. Your mouth really shouldn't move, I tell him, Moving lips is for babies not seven-year-olds. I'm eight, he says. Well, moving lips is certainly not for eight year olds. I suck on my cigarette. When did you become eight? Two weeks ago, he says. Is that right? Well, happy birthday. I tell him, In any case, I say, What does Edmund want? The boy looks up from the paper. I think he wants us to meet him. My heart plunges. I look at the red end of my cigarette. Is that so? And what else? The boy looks back at the letter. Edmund is staying with his mother, he says. Mother, I say. What mother? I stand up, then sit down, repeating *What mother* over and over. And then again. Edmund doesn't have a mother, I say, snatching the letter; perhaps the boy skipped over some long words. But it is just as the boy has dictated. *I am at my mother's, join me here at your earliest convenience.* He has spelled the word convenience wrong. This takes several minutes to overlook. The misspelled word seems to both represent and actually *be* the very worst thing Edmund has done to either of us. I scrape back my chair. At our earliest *conveenence?* I shout. Ordinarily I do not like to shout on account of my fragile vocal cords. I prefer to conserve my vocal cords in case I ever choose to pursue a career in singing. I would not like to spend my life shouting only to find that I have put to rest any hopes of a musical career. After several subdued exhortations, I stop pacing. Where the hell does she live? I ask. Edmund's brother scrutinizes the letter and the envelope. Oh for God's sake, I say, He didn't put an address, did he? The boy shakes his head. I walk to the oven and, bending, place my head on the stovetop. It is the clearest way to indicate my utter helplessness in the face of Edmund's idiocy. From this position it occurs to me I should have placed my head against the refrigerator. The stove is closer to the ground than I anticipated, thereby forcing me to bend lower than I care to, on the whole. A moment passes. I'm stuck, I say finally. I appear to be stuck in this right angle. I hear the boy's chair scrape back and then feel his hands tug me at the waist. We back up together slowly. The boy cannot resist a little *beep beep* as he guides me into a chair. With some pain, I straighten upright. Now, I say, Since Edmund's mother is also your mother, you must know where she lives. The boy sighs. But she's not my mother, he says. I look at him carefully, first straight on, then out of the corner of my eye. Is that the truth? I ask, Because if it isn't, I'm afraid that the consequences could be severe. My patience has come to the end of its tether. I do not know whether patience has a tether or a rope or whether it is itself a rope that frays from overuse, but I have about had it. How like Edmund, I say, How like the genius who goes by the name Edmund. The boy stands and walks out. I'm going to bed, he calls back. Fantastic, I say. Fantastic idea to get your eight hours in. A moment later the corridor light snaps off. Fantastic, I murmur, entranced by the word, Completely fantastic.

Edmund's brother is nearly asleep when I creep into his bed. Shove over, little one, I say, pushing him. Go away, he mutters. But I won't. Look, I say with the spirit of adventure, Help me decode Edmund's strange letter. See how the postmark has blurred several letters in the town name. Help me determine, is there an Italian town called *Litome* or *Letoni* or perhaps *Lidomi?* Go to sleep, the boy says, waving his hand in the air where it chances to smack me in the face. Ow, I say loudly but even that won't wake him. Ensuring that a good amount of the covers stay with the boy, I roll over to face the wall. In the dusky light I trace the letters of our address, which Edmund penned some time last week. He spelled my name right. Though Edmund left out the specifics of how we are to reach him, he did spell my name right and for that I am grateful. In the distance, anarchic strains of organ music, odd and atonal. Schoolboys sneaking in to eulogize. Laughter, drunks on their way home. The shadow of an anemic city tree caught against the moonlight. I used to stare at the wall of my bedroom when I was a girl waiting for sleep. After stories in front of the fire, patient Sally and her insipid adventures, at least before Sally fell into the flames and was eaten to ashes. Then to bed, to choose my dreams before they came, for the ones that arrive on their own accord are too disturbing. Muffled creaks from downstairs as my parents locked doors against the night. It was intolerable of my parents not to have organized a sibling. How different my life would have been with a red-haired sibling to distract my parents or catch a thrown ball. Instead my uncaught tennis balls lay rotting in the cow-weed. It was just me and Sally and Sally's infernal pony. I had no time for Sally, who slipped into the fire one day. Funny how her pages turned bright so quickly even Father could not save her. Father found Sally's immolation deeply suspect. There would be no more books. Quickly thereafter my aunt began to die and the halcyon days of childhood screeched to an end. Edmund's brother flops onto his back with a sigh. Hundreds of telescopes, I hear him mutter, Which would you like to see?

A week later we are officially out of money. We can no longer pay for our rooms. We are so desperate we stop by Toby's café hoping for some sympathy, a surprise letter or a few stale pastries and some milk. But Toby only works two days a week now, they say. They say he attends night courses at the university. We ransack our rooms, pulling up mattresses and digging in the sofa cushions. The boy happens on a stash of vitamins and we swallow them ravenously without checking whether they are D, C or E. I find several coins trapped behind the wardrobe and we buy a round of bread and some cheap prosciutto, marbled with fat. We eat on a grassy slope across from the train station café where we laughed so gaily only weeks before. Remember the day, I begin, but the boy interrupts me. Yes, he says, unusually glum, Yes, he sighs, The day I drank two cups of coffee, I remember it. I stare at him; his eyes have turned piggy and mean. I hope you are never seventeen, I tell him as I help myself to the last of the bread. The boy clutches his stomach. I'm still hungry, he moans, I've been hungry for a week. Many great men suffered from hunger, I say, standing to brush crumbs from my coat, Do you hear their complaints in literature? I think not, I think that rather you read their great thoughts on the matter of Nature, unless of course their complaints make a sort of literature which, to be frank, Sir, yours do not. Your complaints are neither unique nor poetic. I stop because the boy has fainted and I am forced to acknowledge we have a problem of sorts.

Back in our rooms I lead the boy into the sitting room, tuck him under a blanket on the sofa, light a cigarette and begin to pace. First I ask him whether he knows where he sits. He tells me yes, on the lavender sofa on the Piazza Navona. The reason I ask, I say, Is because you fainted out there on the city streets. I point out the window with my cigarette, contorting my face so he will understand just how dangerous it is to become vulnerable on the city streets. Now, I say, I have had a chance to think while you were sleeping and several things have occurred to me. Number one, it occurs to me that we are out of money. Number two, we have been led into some sort of game, some kind of elaborate prank with this Edmund character. I am suddenly feeling very much like a detective and cannot seem to stop myself from speaking in a clipped patois. Number three, since we cannot rely on the reappearance of this *Edmund,* we will have to set aside our dream of owning a science shop. Number four, we are on the verge of being thrown out of our rooms for nonpayment of the rent. I pause to draw a deep inhalation on my cigarette. Yes, a detective would pause; he would smoke a pipe and pace with longer strides than I like to take for the sake of balance. I would have enjoyed being a detective, aside from the wool cloak that is. I have tremendously sensitive skin and can only wear the softest of fibers; the abrasive quality of wool might prove intolerable. If an exception were granted and I did not have to wear wool, there would still be the unfortunate tartans of that office to consider. I could not commit such violence to my character. Some things are not worth the risk, tartan being one. Edmund's brother looks at me expectantly. Number four, I continue. No, the boy interrupts, Not number four, number *Five.* I turn, halfway to the window. Five? I say, Are you certain? He nods. Very well, I say, Better to end on five anyway. Number five and my conclusion: I will have to find employment. What? The boy says. I puff on my cigarette. I see no other way, I tell him. No, he cries, smacking his palm down on the cushion next to him. Well, I'm afraid so, I say, surprised by his athletic reaction to the news. And if it involves a fantastic outfit, so much the better but the fact remains that I will have to work if we're to stay here. Grumpily, the boy kicks his heels against the sofa. What about Edmund? he asks, I thought we were going to find Edmund's mother. Now how the hell do we go to an unnamed place, an addressless spot? I ask. The boy sticks out his lip. So we're never leaving Rome? he says plaintively. You make it sound like our life is hell, I say. Is our life that hellish? He shrugs. Maybe Toby knows where Edmund is, he says. Don't exhaust me, I say, If that brute knew where Edmund is, do you not think he would take the first opportunity to be rid of us? The corners of the boy's mouth turn down. The fact must be faced that Edmund does not want us. You do not need an advanced degree in psychology to make four from two and two. There is no address. And that, as they say, is meaningful. It is so like Edmund to write a letter at the exact moment I stopped thinking about him. Wherever Edmund is, it must have struck him like an andiron that I was planning to open a science shop and it was time to send some troublesome missive to stir the waters.

I find I am clenching my teeth so tightly my jaw is trembling. Yes, like some dolphin reading underwater signals, like a whale tuned to the yawing of another, Edmund raised his head in the middle of his labor and thought, I must send some troublesome letter her way. I stop at the bookcase and pick up a tour guide to Berlin. I pace over to the window; the pigeon man has his shutters open; back to the bookcase to replace the tour guide to Berlin, over to the front door to fiddle with the lock. This is all my fault, I say, I am a vile woman. I stub out my cigarette, I have done vile things, both to a husband and a favored cat and now I am being taught a lesson. Edmund's brother crosses his arms, Oh, not this again! he cries. I ignore him. This is the way with the universe, I continue, We pay for our mistakes, if not at the moment of committing them, then after we die when we are re-born as vermin. But I am being punished during my very lifetime, I tell him, See this as a warning, it could happen to you. No matter how well I treated Edmund I am to be punished for my past. It would not have taken much to avoid this punishment, I continue, I could have worn the dresses provided by my old German husband, I could have worn them in a ladylike fashion instead of slashing at a hem when it caught me in a bad temper. I might have crossed my legs and enjoyed my husband's thoughts on civilization. Instead I sat in a way that had men begging me to leave my sandwiches. It wouldn't have taken much to avoid this punishment, I repeat because I like an incantation. What would it have taken? The brother has buried his head in his hands. I'll tell you what. It would have taken a smile now and then, a little good cheer, some boiled bratwurst when he came home, a stein of warm beer by the pool at night, not much in other words, I shout, Hardly anything in fact. I am not pacing, I am holding a spot by the window, the light against my back. To the boy I must appear a large and alarming silhouette. Instead, I say, lowering my voice a notch so as to avoid expulsion from our rooms, Instead I chose to do it *my own way*. My advice, I tell the boy, My advice to you is never to do things *your own way*, because you'll be ditched with an old sock. Fall in line seems to be the message, I hiss at the boy, Or be guaranteed a life of solitude. He picks up his head and yawns theatrically. My gracious, am I boring you? I ask nicely. The boy rolls his eyes. Then, with the exactitude we notice in the very young and mistake for charm, he reiterates slowly, But. Edmund. Wants. Us. Back. Oh, really? I say. Well, if he wants us back, I ask, Why. Has. He. Not. Provided. Us. With. An. ADDRESS? *Because*, the boy's voice rises half an octave, Because Edmund is stupid! I turn on my heel. How dare you, I hiss. How dare you speak that way of your brother? The boy points at me, But *you* think he's stupid, he cries. Put down your hand at once, I say, cringing with embarrassment though we are alone. The boy breathes quickly in and out of his nose. I don't want you to work, he says, Who will take care of me? I pull out a cigarette. I must say I think you're being incredibly selfish, I say, striking a match. How do you think I feel? Do you think I want to work? It's not like I can command a top teller spot in Rome, just like that. I am not up on the latest procedures and I'm hardly the girl I once was. If you think teller positions in Rome are given to women with rib cages on which you could pluck out a tune, you've been sadly misled. So what am I left with? It's not like I'm good at anything. The boy seems depressed by this comment. We both know it to be true, though

the boy finds it sadder than I do. My secret weapon is being un-
derestimated. When the time comes I will burn away, leave the
world coughing in my exhaust. I puff at the cigarette and put up
my hair. The blood pulses at my temples, from nicotine or the
tightness of my ponytail. We have come to our utmost degrada-
tion. How lucky we are, I tell the boy, Some will never know
what the bottom feels like. Edmund's brother puts a finger on
his cheek; he hasn't done so in months. I don't want you to
work, he says, pouting. God bless, I say exhaling, Some day
you'll make a fine husband for the lazy slut you choose to
marry, but today is not that day, I am not that slut and you are
not my husband. You are eight years old, too young to be sent
into the world of legitimate occupation, though I've thought
about it, believe me. In short, your desires mean less than nothing. If you have something helpful to add to the discussion of
our future please do so, if not, leave me in peace to find a way to
bring meats to the table and milk to your pretty bowl. With
that I go into the back bedroom and begin rifling through my
dresses.

A moment later, the boy follows, climbing up onto the bed
and sucking his finger. Would you like to sing for me? I ask
nicely. He shakes his head. It's a once-in-a-lifetime opportunity,
I say. Meanwhile I am dressing in a way to suggest things but
not demand them; that is, to display some leg without appear-
ing to have left my morals by the side of some road. The delicate balance is making me crazy. The boy lies in bed, moodily

watching me pin and tuck my skirts. Okay, I say, petting his head. Go to sleep until I return.

My heels make a confident clicking noise as I cross the courtyard to our landlord's rooms. I am not certain what to ask for, or what to offer for that matter. I know the rent is due; I know we have no money to pay this rent which is due. But my poppy dress has saved me on many an occasion. It will not fail me tonight. On this night even the moon is uncharitable; only a bitter sliver lights my way across the courtyard. What a grim time. Me who thought I'd end up by the ocean enjoying a glass of exotic fruit juice. Where is the nearest ocean if I could smell its good saltiness right now or observe the practical way the ocean attacks its daily chore of tides and waves, I believe I would be quite the better for it. A vast body of water to replace the smell of rotting, that would certainly be a treat.

At my knock the dark head of Mr. Marcolini appears behind the door's frosted glass. In the shadows I unfasten another button at my décolletage. There is no point in pretending I am above such things. I do not have an ample bosom but that is a deficiency the widower need not discover. I am advertising only. I have no intention of making good on the promotion. Mr. Marcolini gently bows then stands aside to let me pass.

The Marcolini manse contains several statues of exciteable virgins. I pause to examine one as he leads me toward the sitting room. This short maiden appears to be exclaiming, something about her virtue perhaps. I touch her little nervous fingers that reach to heaven. What are you made of? I wonder, because she is so white. He is a rich man, this landlord of ours.

Within minutes the widower is pouring two large Valpoli- cellas and I am toasting him with a twinkle and a flash of cross- ing legs. Marcolini installs a waltz on the turntable's circle of felt. I bend my head to the wine, suddenly afraid he may ask me to dance. If Mr. Marcolini asks me to dance, if I am forced to be close to his tremendous nose, I could very well begin to scream uncontrollably. This happens sometimes, these mo- ments of hysteria coming from who knows where. It is possi- ble that a man with a massive nose played some trick on me during childhood which, in failing to humor me, traumatized me instead. Marcolini snaps his fingers, perhaps in time to the music. I have no idea how music works with its chaotic rules. I bend my head to the wine again. The man's age and large snout are a trying combination. Snap snap, goes Mr. Marcolini. Ex- ternal stimulus is difficult for me tonight. I am nervous and fearful. There is a great deal roiling in my head, from hunger I think. Marcolini beams at me, hunched, snapping his fingers. I carry my wine to the mantel, where a menagerie of small crea- tures clusters together in fear, from a big fire perhaps or drunk hunters. Four fawns graze in a lazy circle. I make them into a strict line of deer ready for inspection. I have made so many bad decisions in this life. A funny thing choice and its bastard cousin free will. Marcolini's small fawns face each other in a menacing square of my own invention. I am not unaware that the widower stares at my bottom as I caper his fawns across the mantel. My custom is to allow the glancing as long as we both understand the other knows about the glancing. Usually I dislike the glancing if the glancing is believed to be furtive. But tonight I don't care that old Marcolini believes I am blind to his glancing. And the music goes on. Okay, time. I turn, I smile. I take an enormous swallow of wine and lift my eyes to the ceiling.

Behind me, something smashes loudly on the floor. Old Marcolini flinches as if he's been struck. I turn to see a fawn has leapt to its death. The music continues, a march, not a waltz as I first thought. On a three-quarter count, I fall to my knees and begin ushering the suicide's broken body into my palm. There are about a thousand blessed pieces; the thing was fashioned out of some sort of crystal. I sweep until pricks of blood appear on my palm. Finally Mr. Marcolini motions for me to deposit the broken fawn into an ashtray. Sorry, I say. Marcolini nods. He has become papal in our short time together. I ignore the ashtray and arrange the shattered deer into piles beginning with the best preserved: a leg, half the head, an entire hindquarter, moving in size down to fragments that are not much more than dust. I become extremely methodical when I am nervous. Stepping back, I assess my composition, brushing my hands together to rid them of any lingering dust. I am quite pleased.

You're very good at that. Marcolini's voice is ripe and at my shoulder. I step away, taking care not to glance in the direction of his nose. I like order, I say without turning. I take another step toward the doorway. Had we met when I was a girl you would have noticed that every object had its special place, I tell my landlord when I am close enough to make a break for the door and tear across the courtyard. The boy has his instructions; if he hears screaming he is to charge at the door while quickly ascertaining whether to bar it or throw it open. As a girl I loved nothing more than to catalogue my possessions, I continue. Though they were few in number they were great in meaning. Not that I was *obsessed*, I say. I can't think anyone would call me a fetishist. But when one has limited means, one worships accordingly. Marcolini advances in my direction with the wine bottle; I take two steps back, holding my glass between us. Yes, he murmurs soothingly, pouring. I watch the level rise in my glass. I worked in a bank once, I say feebly. He looks into my eyes, those watery green windows. I'm sure you did, he says. Encouraged, I confess I once had many skills. Marcolini tells me he had always guessed as much.

Finally I put down my glass. Mr. Marcolini, I say, leaning forward, Dear landlord, how pleasant this evening has been. How delightful. I think perhaps I am leering; I am trying to suggest my proposal instead of using language, to say in some manner, Help. I have always been proud, it is one of my flaws. Yes, it was nice, he says. You must visit me again. Yes, yes, I say, crossing to a monstrous piece of furniture: a sidetable with many drawers. This looks heavy, I say, scrutinizing the wood.

Five candlesticks of varying height stand on its surface. I arrange the tapers in order of height. I assess my décolletage, then turn. About the rent, I say boldly, We cannot pay it the usual way, that is, the boy and I, we have no money. He looks at my chest, then at my hand where it rests on a candlestick. Aha, he says. A proposition.

We are *archivists*, I tell Edmund's brother as we leave Marcolini's kitchen after breakfast. And because we are archivists, we are clean, prompt and exact, always. I noticed something about you this morning, I continue, Something I believe you would want brought to your attention. The boy pushes open the door to the library, looking back at me. It stands to reason that we bring the same meticulous qualities to cooking breakfast for our landlord as we would bring to cataloguing his collection of hideous treasures, I say. The boy nods, passing me a starched white apron I found in the pantry and appropriated for our archival needs. We like to tie the aprons extremely tightly, wrapping the string around our waists several times to convey order and cleanliness by our stark profiles. You have always operated the toaster efficiently, though it means standing on a chair to do it, I tell him. In fact I have quietly admired the devotion you bring to the slicing of bread, the insertion of it into the toaster, how you gain purchase on the side of the sink in order to throttle the bread down into the machine, and yet. And yet, I continue, This morning, crumbs were scattered across the floor, the butter knife was never cleaned and I noted a shoeprint left behind on your kitchen chair. I trust this slovenly behavior will remain confined to the breakfast room, I say. Please don't bring it here, to our archival chamber. Wordlessly Edmund's brother goes to one of the enormous cupboards that line the walls of Marcolini's study. Then, keeping his back to me, he says, I didn't see any crumbs. I watch him open a drawer and take out the next object in the sequence of horrific objects we spend our days archiving for old Marcolini. Fine, I say. Perhaps I was having some sort of delusion and there were no crumbs, I'm certain everything was exactly as it was yesterday. Sometimes I let him have his little opinions.

The boy brings the next of our landlord's objects to the examining table. I position the gooseneck lamp over it and we watch as he slowly peels away layers of tissue paper. When the last piece of paper comes away, we both take a step back. The boy averts his eyes. Good God, I say, stunned. The teapot is grotesque. What was wrong with that woman? the boy says. We have yet to satisfactorily diagnose the dead wife's aesthetic disorder. Had someone handed us a lump of clay we could have fashioned a thing far less ugly, I say. *Hé bien, la guerre.* Onward. I assess the teapot, pencil pleasantly rapping my temple. Rococo? asks the brother. No, I say, While the theme of lovers lounging in a garden is certainly Rococo, this is not an original. Look here, I motion with my pencil. See the encrusted flowers here and here? That seems more a Victorian affect to me. I reach for my cigarettes, pulling one out of the packet with my teeth, all the while keeping my eyes riveted to the disgusting object, hypnotized by its swarming roses and vines. Meissen, the boy says, looking up from the reference book, Circa. Eighteen eighty-two. He strikes a match, lights my cigarette, then swiftly pulls on a pair of white gloves and sets about cleaning the vase with a particularly noxious fluid.

On our first day, the boy unwrapped a porcelain terrier with a clock for intestines and we fell on the floor laughing at the poor thing's useful stomach. We have had a great deal of laughter at our landlord's expense. But when we hear Marcolini's sabots in the corridor outside the library the boy and I never laugh. At these moments we press our lips together and look very, very stern and hold things up to the light.

After lunch the boy and I spend an hour reading love letters written by an admiral over one hundred years ago. Today we have reached the end of the salty dog's letters. I am glad the captain stopped when he did with those letters, I tell Edmund's brother. We are fat with fruit and impatient with the Admiral's tedious description of sea and weather, with the unending greyness of his fog. How bored we are by his unrequited longing. How could fog be anything but grey, I ask you, I say when we have reached the last of his correspondence. Edmund's brother strokes his stomach idly, a faraway look on his face. I wonder if the captain ever saw Esmé again, he says, Maybe she married another man while he was away at sea. Maybe she married that piano player, he continues, She described her piano lessons in every single letter. Hardly, I say, organizing our peach pits and cherry stones into small piles because now I organize everything. Really, I think not. I think this dull Esmé would not have saved letters from a man she betrayed. My hunch is she would not have wanted the Admiral's letters hanging around the place making her feel terrible. I think rather, the old man died at sea. The boy looks over at me. Murdered by pirates? he asks. Quite, I say. This seems to please him; he goes back to stroking his bloated stomach. Although it is equally plausible his own crew turned mutinous out of sheer boredom, I add, standing up. I shuffle the Admiral's letters, organizing them by date and slipping them into plastic covers. Esmé kept the letters because he drowned, I say, What a sad tale. Perhaps we are wrong to mock the poor Admiral who had only scurvy-addled mates and the scent of putrefied mutton to keep him company all his days at sea. The brother stands up. But it could have been pirates, he says, There's no way to know. I hand the boy the love letters. Fine, I tell him, As you wish. The boy takes the letters to the filing case. What do you think Edmund would say if he saw us now? he asks, turning back to me. *Edmund?* I say, winking, Was that his name?

Dear Edmund. Though you left us for vagrants without a second thought, your brother and I have become famous archivists. You thought we were worthless but we have proven you wrong. You thought we would suffer your disappearance;

that was a faulty assumption on your part. We have been working for Mr. Marcolini, our ancient landlord, and are much changed. We travel in the best company; eat rich foods and are treated like royalty in the fine shops of Rome where we make our many purchases.

But we don't, the boy says. We still don't have any money and we never eat supper. I light a cigarette, sit back and put my feet up on Marcolini's desk. Well I'm not planning on *sending* the damn letter, I tell the boy, removing a piece tobacco from my tongue and examining it before flicking it aside. As you are aware, there is nowhere to send a letter to your brother but orbit. One hundred years ago and at sea, the Admiral could remark how grey the ocean gets; you and I are not so fortunate.

Edmund has been gone for nearly three months by my calendar the evening I pull on my poppy dress and slip a few lire up my sleeve. When I close the wardrobe door, the boy is standing behind it with folded arms. I jump, startled. Must you creep up on people like that? I say, turning to the dressing table. Where are you going? he asks. I pick up my brush and begin to run it through my hair vigorously. Where are you going? he repeats. I heard you the first time, I say, fastening a hair clip, And the answer is nowhere; I am going nowhere. You don't brush your hair for *nowhere,* the boy says gravely. I glare at him in the mirror, Why don't you run along and get into bed where it's nice and warm and no one will accidentally deal you a slap? I'll be along in a moment to make certain no ogres lurk behind the door. I kneel to search under the bed for my shoes. I don't believe in ogres, he says stubbornly. Vampires, then, I say. Silence. I stand up holding a shoe. The boy hasn't moved. No such thing as vampires, he mutters. Fine, I tell him, Forget about the monsters, just get into bed. The boy stays still, his mouth turned down. Does everything have to be so serious? I ask. My God, when did it all get so bloody grim? I am exhausted by your seriousness, I say, And frankly, your brother was no better. Your brother, for all his vacuity, loved nothing more than to hunker down over some *serious* issue that I never found serious at all. In fact usually the opposite was true. It was typically the case that whatever made your brother frown and pinch his eyebrows together made me laugh like the devil. Thankfully your brother is no longer with us and I no longer have to bear his depressing gravity. Because these days I am finding that the one thing I can live without is the high-minded self-importance of people like you. You, I say, using my shoe as a pointer, Are becoming dull. I raise my eyebrows, driving home the seriousness of the remark, and bend to my feet. But you can't just leave me here alone, he says. I am hooped over, trying to force my foot into my shoe, at the end of my breath and patience. Oh, I most certainly can, I tell him upside down. What if there's a fire? the boy asks, What if the police arrive and find me dead in the ashes?

Duchess *of* Nothing

My foot will not fit in my shoe and I am forcing it even though it hurts like hell. Oh for God's sake, I say, stamping my foot. Why are you like this? Like what? he asks, Eight? I continue stamping my foot. Yes, I say, Like eight. Like eight, like seven, at me night and day like some sort of toothache, never a moment's peace. How can I have a mind of my own when your mind is always there too? And don't sigh, I tell him, I am tired of the sighing. I am tired of the milk and frying your onions and you always needing everything. How can I think as I really think when you hover around robbing me of my soul? Edmund's brother goes to the dressing table and holds up a string of cheap pearls. Can I wear these? he says. I turn my eyes to the ceiling to call on any higher power. I open my mouth and scream though no sound comes out. Then I stop. So, you're saying I'll feel depressed if you die? I ask quietly, leveling my gaze, You're saying I have to take you out dancing with me in case I come home tonight drunk with ecstasy only to find you lying on the floor stiff as a board? I'm clarifying, I say, Is that the case? The boy nods happily, the pearls now roped around his neck. You never know, I say, I might just step over you and go straight to bed, overjoyed to find I might wake in the morning and not boil any damn milk. You wouldn't be glad, he says confidently, drawing a mustache above his lip with my eyebrow pencil. Look, he says, turning. I look. Now there's a sense of fashion for you, I say. He smiles and I can see he has also blackened one of his front teeth. I sigh. You're a real joy, aren't you? I ask, A real bloody joy.

The boy sits at the bar, high on a bar stool sipping wine diluted with water, kicking his feet in time to the music while I dance like a maniac. But I cannot stop, I am free from the rabbit catchers, even Edmund, from the tight wires strung between us. We are free, now, the boy and I.

At the end of the song, I return to the bar. Give me a gin, I tell the bartender, dabbing my forehead to cool myself. This is good, I tell the boy, Isn't it? I look around the crowded joint, hectic and warm. It's alright, he says. Come on, I say, lifting him down from his stool, Time to dance. And so we go, we dance. The music is accordions and flutes, some Latin singer with flashing eyes. No one notices the boy is eight years old and not a midget. We are having the very best time, I cry, though I hate any announcement of a good time. When a good time is announced I immediately begin to have a very bad time. But nothing can mar our good time, we spin, we love our lives, my very big life and the boy's somewhat smaller one. Because for the brother and me, there is no need for Edmund's back, no need for Edmund at all. I don't wait for anyone, I shout at the boy. And it requires no pliancy of the imagination to observe that we are far better off without that malcontent. Drunk is good, though I am not drunk, it is just that everything is velvety, the world has its edges softened, and for once I am quite glad I am myself and no one else. I forget everything and hours later when my teeth begin to hurt we stumble home. Or I stumble, weaving, my elbow propped on the boy's head, telling my boy bloody everything.

Several cloudy hours later it is very difficult to make it downstairs to Marcolini's. Impossible. I am lying down, I call to the boy on hearing him fumble in the toilet at some point, perhaps late afternoon. I am having a lie-down before dinner, I tell him. Edmund's brother appears in the doorway with his fly unzipped. Will you fix yourself, I ask, averting my gaze to the ceiling as I motion toward his crotch, Or were you planning to proposition Rome this afternoon? My peripheral vision is faulty but I can make out the quick drop of his head, the clumsy arrangements. There are many ways to describe this but I am not in the mood right now. To avoid thinking creatively, I make a blank of my mind. It is difficult to conceive unending blankness so I imagine I am staring very closely at a white wall. The boy has finished his zipping but remains in my doorway. We can't stay here all day, he says. Absolutely we can stay here all day, I tell him, Many important men spent their entire lives in bed examining train schedules. We call this contemplation, I say, and it goes without saying that had Melville been forced to boil milk every other minute, he would have had no time to think about any fat whale, white or otherwise. I fall back onto the pillow, exhausted. Silence. I roll my eyes over to him. Edmund's brother is still staring at me. I hold up a pillow to deflect his intense gaze. I'm hungry, he says. Are you going to faint again? I ask curiously from behind the pillow. No, he says grumpily, But I want meat, I can't eat any more vegetables. It is true that the day before, while crossing the Piazza Navona, a man dropped half his panino. It is also true that the boy and I fell on the meat like dogs. I recall this but I do not mention it. I say, Many people the world over grow healthy on vegetables. These people call themselves vegetarians and swing their hands by their sides as they smugly skip around spiders. In some countries, I add, You will find religion forbids eating a pig or cow. Eat a pig or cow in certain hot countries and you'll be smote by a god; not our god, mind you, but their god. And perhaps not just one god, but many gods, each with several arms. Then I turn over, flipping the pillow and smoothing the sheets that I might fall asleep without the irritation of any lumps. I sigh, burying my head in the fresh side of the pillow. Imparting lessons from bed, a first. I really think you might take notes, I say, lifting my head to look at him. I spent Edmund's hard-earned money on a green notebook, would it kill you to make some use of it? The boy doesn't move. Go away, please, I say. But the boy remains standing in the bedroom doorway. Abraham killed his son, I mention, When ordered to by God. The boy doesn't move. There was a time years ago, perhaps just on the cusp of the anno domini, that children obeyed orders, I say. During the time people wore bark-colored shifts. I have always liked those shifts; they seem particularly comfortable, I add, At least from the paintings. A pause. My joints hurt, the boy says moodily. Oh for God's sake, I shout, Are we still carping on about this? We're the proverbial dog at the bone on this one, are we? But, the boy stammers, I might have a protein deficiency. I am up in a flash. *Joints? Protein? Deficiency?* I am up and sitting on the edge of the bed, my head joining my body several seconds later. I collect myself, vow there will be no more alcohol, or at least less of it and point at the boy like God. Our god, the one who points. How do you know words like *protein deficiency?* A dreadful silence. Mercifully it is short. Have. You. Been. *Reading?* I ask slowly. The boy's bottom lip trembles. I jump up but am forced to remain unsteadily hunched for a few minutes with bent knees. After a minute I feel the boy's small paw on my back. Oh, I don't think so, I say, righting myself and sweeping past him. I march down the corridor. Loudly, for effect. Unfortunately this makes my head feel as if it is being smashed by a ball-peen hammer. In the living room, all is as usual. The carpet remains scattered with the boy's building bricks, there is no sign of any reading material. The room is its same dark self, the sordid smell, the fading furniture, two black tables turning brown. I remain in the doorway, huffing. I trust I won't find any outside influences in here, I tell Edmund's brother lurking somewhere behind me. You know how vulnerable you are to toxic opinions. All those opinions scattered in the breeze just waiting for you to ingest them; it breaks my blessed heart. I stride to the window. The courtyard below is empty. I turn back to him. You may have your own thoughts when you are capable of crossing a street alone, I tell Edmund's brother. For now, I say, For now you are to follow my course of study, the one I carefully prepare every day, or at least some days. I stare down at the wretched child. I know if I wait long enough he'll give the game away. A minute later his gaze shifts and I pounce, yanking up the sofa cushion and pulling out a newspaper. An international gazette, no less. When I am very angry, I get quiet, but when I am furious I cannot speak at all. With no small amount of drama I begin to page through the news. An article on city planning, one on theater offerings, international news, and here on page seven, a small item on protein deficiency in growing children. The boy stands on one leg like a river bird. Finally I find the words. Where did this come from? He looks behind him. It didn't come from behind you, I say. He mutters. I beg your pardon? Mr. Marcolini, he says, Mr. Marcolini gave it to me. Oh, Mr. Marcolini *gave* it to you? I say to verify that I have heard him correctly. He nods. It's in English, I say. Did he buy it for you, especially for you? The boy nods. Ah, I say. And did you *ask* him to buy it for you? He shrugs. Stay here, I say brightly, nearly adding a politely British, *won't you?* As I do when I am angry, become Anglified. I slide my feet into my buckle shoes that stand by the door. Please don't, the boy says, pulling on my arm as I buckle my shoes. Don't *please don't* me, I say, I have been charged with your education, moral, spiritual and intellectual, not Mr. Marcolini our

decaying landlord who collects spoons and locks them in cupboards. Mr. Marcolini has stepped outside the bounds of our
arrangement. Clearly he needs to be reminded of what that
arrangement is. There is nothing to be upset about, I say soothingly, Though I could not have been less happy had I caught you
ogling naked tarts. I smooth my dress; by coincidence it belonged to the late Mrs. Marcolini. This gives me pause. I pause
with my hands in mid-smoothing, consider the dress, consider
my options, consider the boy, then turn on my heel, slam the
front door behind me and take the stairs two at a time.

Mr. Marcolini is sitting in his armchair, his mouth wide
when I slam the door behind me. He does not wake so I open
the door and slam it again with more force. In my right hand I
grip the offensive pages; my left hand now holds the doorknob,
which has come off in my hand. He wakes up. Mr. Marcolini, I
say loudly, What is this? His eyes flick open. I identify egg yolk
lodged in a molar. Mr. Marcolini confirms my fears. Ah, a *newspaper,* I repeat. An international newspaper. Now I begin to
pace. Mr. Marcolini, what are our arrangements? I ask rhetori-
cally. I must admit, I am thoroughly enjoying myself. It is seldom that I am both certain I am right and justified in shouting
about it. This is one of those rare occasions and I cannot deny
myself a simultaneous pace and shout. As Mr. Marcolini re-
views our arrangements, I pace back and forth from mantel to
window to door all the while forcing Marcolini to look behind

his back to locate me or contract his failing sight to find me against the bright afternoon. As I pace I enjoy assuming the curt nods and pressed lips of the legal profession. I try some variations of lip presses and come to favor a contorted pout I deem quite French. I only wish he had a Souza playing. Finally the widower stops speaking. I allow Mr. Marcolini's last words to hang in the air for a minute; now I hold the evidence aloft. And this? I bray, Where does this fit into our arrangements? Marcolini smiles. Oh, he says, I gave that to the boy free of charge. Our landlord sits in a luxurious armchair with wide arms. I imagine the wide arms of my landlord's armchair are exceptional for balancing plates of biscuits while you lounge by the fire sampling biscuits and oppressing the working classes. I lunge forward and kneel on one of the arms of his armchair. It's a limber and surprising move, not to mention menacing. I need to be close to Marcolini to impress upon him the gravity of his mistake. I hope that if Marcolini ever thinks to hand the boy some reading material again, he will recall my looming visage and let the offending pages slide to the floor. Mr. Marcolini, I say, Let me make myself clear. Don't. Do not give my charge books, newspapers or dictionaries. Do not give him magazines, brochures, periodicals, advertisements, bibles or . . . I trail off, stumped. In short, I say, raising my voice, He is an eight-year-old child with an impressionable mind and I will not have it corrupted with your filth. He is mine, I shout,

And I will do with him what I will! Mr. Marcolini clutches his
chest. We stare at each other. We are very close and very silent.
I reach out and gently pick a crumb from his cardigan. This I
inspect, then place to one side. Mr. Marcolini sits, silently
white. I set down the newspaper, now nicely folded, on a low
table and place the doorknob beside it. I trust I have made my
point, sir. With that, I turn on my heel, pulling Marcolini's
door behind me as I go. It is my misfortune that the other
knob, the exterior knob, comes off in my hand. I am so intoxi-
cated from shouting that it takes a minute to understand what
it is I am holding. I stare at the knob with astonishment. Then
I set it down next to the door and whistling, cross the courtyard toward the rooms I share with Edmund's brother. As I begin to climb the stairs, it dawns on me that I have in effect
entombed our landlord in his rooms.

The boy sees my worried expression as soon as I enter.
Obediently he gives me the information that yes, yes indeed we
left Mr. Marcloini with enough resources to make dinner and
yes, yes enough wine too should he like to spend another evening attacking his liver. Still I am distressed. To return would
mean to lose the drama of my exit. My memories mean everything to me; much more than the experience itself, which cannot be altered while one is having it. The memory of my speech
to Marcolini, which was not only lucid, but quite justified,
promises to be especially rewarding. Yet the man is surely too
arthritic to enjoy an alternate exit. I look at the boy searchingly,

with the same searching eyes I once turned toward my cat. But the boy only returns that moggy's vacant look. I could send the boy to Marcolini's, yes, yes, he can squeeze his small frame in through one of the windows or wedge a knife in the lock. On the other hand I could wait until morning, so as not to disturb the memory of my invigorating shout. The boy has replaced the cushion I snatched from the sofa; he is now staring glumly at his sandals, which he has taken to wearing day and night. We labor for better, I say. We labor for better. With that, I return to the bedroom.

The room could use a dust I notice. There is much to review. Mr. Marcolini's blank face, it was very white when I left. Had I shouted too loudly? I try to recall if Marcolini had eaten breakfast that morning with his usual hearty appetite. He had not forced on us his usual soporific tales, no, he had spoken only once and then with a softness that was uncharacteristic. He asked that perhaps his toast might be a bit darker, he found it slightly rare, he said, and he liked it to be crisp when he bit it. He enjoyed the shower of fine crumbs, he preferred toast, he whispered, not warm bread. And then what, I test my short-term memory, then what? Did I turn to Edmund's brother? Yes, yes that was it. I turned to the boy. I said, One job and you make an utter hash of it. A wave of remorse, nausea roils me from head to toe. We labor for better, how rarely we manage. I stagger to my feet, walk clumsily to where the boy still sits, gazing at his sandal, which he taps on the floor. I clear my throat. He raises his eyes to me. I believe I have killed our landlord, I say. I would like to pin the blame on the boy but I can think of no easy way to do it. I sink to my knees. The food is bound to be terrible in prison, I say. Not to mention the lack of freedom. Edmund's brother gets up and sighs, then he walks across the room to where I sit folded oddly against the wall. He puts his sweet, miniature hands one on each side of my head and presses my temples as if to encourage more positive thoughts. Don't think you won't die without me here to look after you, I whisper. He keeps pressing. Unless you get carted off to an orphanage, I add more brightly, Which might not be so terrible. Plenty of literature comes from orphans, I say, No one needs a family to provide thematic material. The boy sits close to me, hesitant to interrupt; he recognizes the speech as my valediction. I have struggled, I tell him, Not to be the person I was born or the person I grew into, but somebody else entirely. Ever since I met your brother in the Alps I have tried to resist being the scourge that left her husband. He only ever wanted his meals at seven fifteen and half past six, along with a smile now and again. But I could not do that for him, I say. I have tried to give you what I was denied at your age, an education, a sense of the world, so that you may grow into an admirable person. In the far distance, the wail of a siren, police or ambulance, perhaps both, one for Marcolini, one for me. In my head I make wild promises as we hear the sound of footsteps on the stairs. The boy puts his hands on my shoulders and stares into my eyes. The footsteps stop outside our door. A knock. The boy and I look at each other. The door handle turns; I open my mouth to scream. The door flies open. We look up, frozen in terror. Edmund.

I wake feeling damned. Below me in his mother's garden Edmund is trying to force his easel upright. As soon as one thin leg gains purchase in the mud, the opposing leg lifts or sinks, making his easel stagger like a drunk. Fool, I say to myself, Asinine fool. Today there isn't a thing I wouldn't do to flee this living hell. I pull a blanket from the bed and slope down the corridor to the boy's room. Well, I woke feeling damned, I announce, settling into the blue armchair and arranging my blanket comfortably about my shoulders. So don't start begging me to crawl under the covers with you this morning, I say, Because I am in no mood. I am in no mood for the needs of little boys. I have woken to adult terrors, specifically to the universe's relentless wish to damn me, and my patience is beyond thin this morning. Besides, I add, I need to sit here to admire your brother's endeavors in the garden and you know how difficult it is to see him from over there. The boy's head emerges from a sea of bedcovers. What time is it? he asks, coughing. Early, I tell him. Damn early. The boy rolls over onto his back, kicking off the covers. He lies splayed like a beached starfish. The boy and I like to lie on our backs and look up. If I am under a tree and well shaded I can even bear a blazing summer sun as long as I am looking up. But I find winter is the season, with its doomed plants, black trees. In winter once, walking along a desolate path, I fell quite purposefully onto my back into eighteen inches of snow. I lay still even as my clothes began to soak through and grow cold. Branches overhead were bowed by snow and though I am not a declarer of beauty, though I like to find beauty where none have found it or in objects that have never been reproduced and sold as trinkets, I admit to a certain surging at the way the white met the dark trees. The moment summoned thoughts of greater good, albeit in the most detached of ways. After a moment a bracing laugh resounded through the forest, that of a hunter perhaps, and I was forced to leave. It has become so difficult, I don't know since when, but it has become so difficult to find a moment of fucking peace.

I light a cigarette. I am gravitating to sadness this morning on account of my damnation, I tell the boy, extinguishing the match with a sad shake. There was a time not so long ago when you used to light my cigarette for me, I add. Do you remember that time in our rooms on the Piazza Navona? Since you are only eight years old that might seem a long time ago, a lifetime ago. I gaze at the cigarette, transfixed by its burning end. Can you imagine waking up to damnation? I ask. Oh the things I regret at night as your brother snores next to me, the smallest of smiles pasted below his nose. You must never grow into that man, I say as I get to my feet and cross to the window, I absolutely forbid it. While I understand that genetic patterns are in place over which neither of us has control, it will still pain me very much if you grow into a stupid man. After all, I say, I have forsaken my own dreams in order to educate you, what a pity if such sacrifice were in vain. The boy turns and hangs his head over the side of the bed. Are you going to vomit? I ask, turning with interest. He shakes his head. Would you like me to get under the covers with you? Again the boy shakes his head. I hope you never feel damned, I say, It's certainly no picnic. Edmund's brother sighs. Well, I say, dousing my cigarette in the cup of milk on the windowsill, At least your brother is having a nice time of it. Look at him out there painting his little masterpieces. In a matter of days, he will have conceived the gardens, the house, even the lane outside. Perhaps he will paint your portrait, if you stop succumbing to these irritating moods all the time. The boy sighs again. I wonder why you're sighing when I'm the one who woke feeling damned, I say. I wonder why you're rolling around huffing like a fat lady in silk pajamas when I'm having such a time of it. It seems fairly selfish if you ask me. We call this *stealing thunder,* I tell him. Stealing thunder is when you rob the moment for yourself instead of having sympathy for a friend's damnation. I don't ask for much, I remind him, But a little kindness from time to time would not go unnoticed. Edmund's brother remains with his head hanging over the edge of the bed, one finger tracing a circular pattern in the mother's revolting carpet. He has been so unusual ever since we arrived at the mother's two months ago. I lean against the window. In this position I can easily see both Edmund below me and, with a slight turn of my head, his brother lolling over the side of the bed. You'll lose the feeling in your feet if you stay that way for long, I say, All the blood will rush to your head and a surgeon will end up having to amputate a leg. I don't know what sort of medical training they have out here in the country but I can't think it's terribly good. Edmund's brother flips onto his back and stares at the ceiling. It's not like I begged to come here, I remind him, pointing my cigarette at the countryside beyond the window, This relentless pastoral wasn't my bloody idea. Can you really believe all this vegetation inspires in me anything but the most profound of depressions? As I recall I was quite content on the Piazza Navona. Finally Edmund's brother pulls back the sheets and gets out of bed. At last, I say, Now we can begin to situate some new ideas in that little head of yours. He crosses to the adjoining bathroom without looking back at me.

Nearly two months have passed since the day Edmund appeared on our doorstep in Rome. As our landlord lay prone in the flat below, number zero zero three, the boy and I packed up our things, jumped in Edmund's car and fled to the country. We would have preferred, the boy and I, to ignore Edmund for several days. We would have loved to see Edmund beg for forgiveness, sob or spread expensive baubles on the kitchen table in an effort to win us back. But fear of prosecution kept us moving. We ran around our rooms, the brother and I, grabbing clothes, his magnifying glass, my butterfly net and our favorite bowl with roses painted on the inside. We collided into each other several times as the boy shouted questions, showed Edmund his sandals and at one point stood stock still and screeched like a parrot for no apparent reason. On the drive to the mother's house we appeared very normal from the outside. Anyone looking at us would have seen a handsome couple motoring in the country with their young boy. Unfortunately nothing clenches my heart with an icy hand as firmly as the appearance of normalcy. I shut my eyes at the sight of every passing car, certain we would be smashed to pieces and I would be destined to appear in the afterlife a normal woman. I have never trusted picnics. What augurs tragedy more clearly than a sandwich cut into triangles and served in wax paper? I grew more and more anxious as I observed Edmund gulping fresh air and swigging enthusiastically from a tartan thermos. Why had he left so suddenly and why had he returned? Where was he taking us? Then, as we drove on through the night, Edmund and his brother began singing popular songs and I began to have very dark thoughts indeed. I became more and more convinced I would be locked in the attic upon arrival.

The car came to the end of a long drive framed by hawthorns and the mother's house rose up as forbidding as any asylum. She appeared the following morning: a hatchet-faced woman with dead eyes at the head of the table. A woman to make you think of dank smells, of earth and turnips and ceaseless cellars beneath her skirts. I suspect Edmund's mother never wakes feeling damned. Despite her dead eyes, I suspect the mother engages in the sorts of charitable activities that stave off damnation; the very ones that make me insane. I imagine that Edmund's mother has a busy schedule attending to society's poor. I cannot abide too many virtues in one vessel. Oh yes, I can see her feeding the community wastrels, a bright smile compensating for those dead eyes. Others might buy it, I think, But not I. Never. I know death when I scent it, in any guise. Edmund's brother comes out of the washroom. Did you wash your hands? I call out. He disappears back into the bathroom, returning a minute later with a sheepish grin. Today we will investigate the sciences, I say. I've noticed your grasp of biology is not what it should be. We should get out into those green spaces before the weather turns and we're hampered by snow. The boy's face falls. What's wrong? What's wrong with biology? I thought you loved the sciences. Edmund's brother shrugs. Remember our

Science Shop? I ask, Remember the snug corner where the leading minds discussed their theories? But the brother has paused
by the window and stands, with one hand on the glass, staring
out at the gardens. What's your brother up to? I ask, crossing to
stand next to him, How's our Michelangelo? Edmund looks up
at the window. He sees us watching and waves. We wave back.
Then he motions to me. Is your brother *beckoning?* I ask the boy,
Or is that some country wave? No, Edmund's brother says, He
wants you to go to him. Very well, I say. Apparently I'm being
beckoned, so I shall go.

    Downstairs, in addition to the blanket wrapped around my
shoulders I pull on a pair of Wellington boots I find by the back
door. It is wearing this ensemble that I greet Edmund. I would
have never left our rooms in Rome with uncombed hair and a
blanket over my nightdress. But we live now in the country,
where women let their hair turn to hay while wearing shoes
that are kind to the feet. Edmund and his easel have brokered
a peace before an unremarkable tree. I am uncertain what
species of tree, an oak perhaps. He has chopped off the fingers
of a pair of gloves and wears them night and day. From this I
glean that fingerless gloves complete the portrait of a landscape
painter that Edmund holds in his mind. The month is October
I think. I am trying to provide the facts I know in the order
they arrive. I may not know the exact type of the tree Edmund
paints, but I am nearly certain that the month is the tenth one

of the year, October. And I believe it is nigh on seven in the morning or perhaps only half past the six.

Here I am, I announce as I approach our great painter. You beckoned? Edmund kisses me on the forehead. I wrap my arms around him. Gently he extricates himself. He looks up at the boy's bedroom. The boy stands where I left him, by the window, watching us. I wish he would see to dressing, I say, I have a full day's education planned and we are falling behind. There is still the milk to boil and the gardener to find. I believe the gardener may have stolen the butterfly net, I say, Which, as you know, once belonged to my father. My father caught many strains of butterflies in that net during his lifetime and I would hate to have it stolen from me. I have precious few mementoes passed down to me and my father's butterfly net is the one I treasure above all others. Edmund squints at me as if I stand in the distance. Perhaps once you begin to paint, every object becomes confused with its background. From Edmund's expression he is suffering from a surfeit of visual stimulus and must squint to determine me. The gardener hasn't taken your net, Edmund says, He is fixing it, merely fixing it. Fine, I say, I am only suggesting we keep an eye on him. I inhale the morning air deeply a few times, then take out a cigarette. What's on your mind? I ask. Edmund sighs. He puts his hands on his hips. He looks to the house, the garden, his canvas and his shoes. He does not look at me. What is it? I ask, Is someone dying? Edmund looks at me. Not exactly, he says. I wait for Edmund to tell me who has died inexactly. If his brother were standing next to me it would be very difficult not to snigger at Edmund's verbal burlesque. I love you, he says suddenly. *What?* I say, choking on my cigarette smoke, You *what?* I begin to laugh but I am coughing so I cough and cough until Edmund is forced to hammer my back with the palm of his hand. When I can breathe again I move several steps away from Edmund to study him. To find him against his background, as it were. He is searching the sky with a look of glazed peace. I follow his gaze to a few scudding clouds. I heard you, I mutter. Yes, I heard him. There are few faculties I trust as much as my hearing. Anyway, Edmund says, turning to me brightly, Did I tell you that I'm planning to sell my paintings? I shake my head, reduced to silence. Yesterday I decided I would sell the watercolors I've been making of Mother's garden in order to bring in some money. I shift from side to side, trying to distribute my weight evenly. There isn't enough money, he says. It's one of the reasons I came here, to help, he says. Even Mother might have to take work, or sell cakes. It is a difficult time, Edmund says, We are all required to make some effort. I nod thoughtfully, my head undone. Fine, I say. Yes. Finally Edmund stops speaking. Well, I say, If you'll excuse me, I have to go educate.

Back in the bedroom, Edmund's brother has spread sheets of newspaper on the mother's ugly carpet and has begun smearing his sandals with thick brown polish. I'm going back to bed,

I tell him, This day is killing me. My constitution is not strong enough to handle the ideas I've heard today, I say, Now I need to stare at a ceiling. Though the mother's ceiling does not have the orgy of cracks offered by our divine ceiling back in the Piazza Navona, still it offers me some sense of peace. What did Edmund say? The brother asks. I am an inch from the bed but instead of getting in, I double back and return to the door. In effect, I begin to pace. I don't know where to begin, I tell the boy, You won't believe this farce, but Edmund tells me he is planning to sell those mysterious canvases he paints. Can you believe it? The boy shakes his head; his eyebrows form a worried V. I know, I say, I know. You see it was never art at all; it was only to avoid getting carted to the poorhouse. It's not that I have anything against helping family though all my family died before I could offer any help, I say, It's this insistence of his own worth. It's the swagger that allows him first to decide to paint though he has no training and second to think that he and he alone can save the household. Do you not think I could save the household if I put my mind to it? Do you not think you could? Of course we could if that's what we *chose* to do. Furthermore, those paintings he makes, do they qualify as art? I ask the boy, Because I am not a person to begrudge a man his art. Mess around with little paints in tubes; did I say a word? Edmund's brother shakes his head. No, I translate, *I never said a word.* When Edmund first began with his up at first light and smudgy smock, I never said a word against it. I thought, here is a man who needs to explore his inner life via a schoolboy's watercolor set, good for him. In reality of course I thought it was asinine. Of course, agrees the boy. *Of course.* And though neither of us said one word to the other, we both knew it to be asinine. But, I hold up a finger to warn the boy against maligning his brother too much, We allow our fellow man to express himself in whatever form that expression takes that is within the bounds of good taste and the law. As we know, I say, edging my thumb under a piece of wood that has separated from the windowsill, Your brother has a feeble vocabulary and a limited intellect. Therefore anything he does to surprise us should be encouraged, anything he does to *branch out* should be greeted with delight, not derision. However. The boy looks up at me from the floor; he can tell I am pointing. However, I repeat, The moment Edmund gets grandiose, which seems to be right this moment, that is a moment to become very annoyed. I think you and I are well within our rights as people with developed intellects and many things to say, to be extremely annoyed. After all, has anyone given us paints? I ask, searching the room for these people. Has anyone bestowed on us a typewriting machine to record the many, many fascinating topics that pass between us on any given day? Edmund's brother shakes his head. No, I interpret, No they have not. I believe they are terrified, I say, though I doubt this somewhat. They are absolutely terrified to hear or see what we have to say or what we have to render. That's how it would provoke the world, I say. I pace to the door

and back to the window and then to the door again. Edmund's
dabblings are going to save us all from the poorhouse, I tell the
brother. Because make no mistake, if Edmund decrees it, so it
will be. If you doubt for one moment that his decision to rake
in a few barrels of bills from scribbling will come to pass, you
are very, very wrong. Edmund's brother delicately plucks some
carpet fluff from his sandal where it has been glued by polish.
He sets the shoe down on the newspaper next to its shiny
brother. My stomach hurts, I say suddenly, collapsing on the
floor, putting my head in the boy's lap. He bends over me; his
hair smells ripe and unwashed. I want to do it too, I say in a
whiny voice. The boy picks up my head with both hands and
moves it gently from his lap to the floor. You want to paint? he
asks, going to my feet and unbuckling my shoes. I don't know, I
say, Something other than this. I let the brother pull off my
shoes. Today has been horrible thus far, I announce. I find I do
not like the smell of this day, not at all. On the whole I am finding damnation very, very tedious. I get up, slouch across the
room and climb into the boy's bed. Edmund's brother pulls the
blanket up to my chin. I like bed very much, I tell him, It might
exhaust me to paint and I have never liked the sun. He pets my
hands tenderly where they emerge from the bedcovers like bird
claws. Painting might require blistering under the hot sun, I
murmur, Yes, I recall seeing photographs of painters. They wear
straw hats, they blister in the sun, and their skin is often bright
and waxy. I could not bear to blister under the sun like that; I

have very delicate skin that burns at the slightest increase in temperature. The boy pushes a water glass on the bedside table closer to me. You're being very nice, I say suspiciously, Have you done something? He shakes his head. I don't think you would like to be a painter, he tells me, I think you would find it hot and boring. I smooth the sheet where it is folded over the blanket. Yes, I say, Though I could easily overcome uncomfortable circumstances in the name of something large and meaningful. That is, after all, the definition of a well-lived life, is it not? We must bear the difficulties in order to reap rewards. The boy nods. It's that mother's doing, I say. I wonder what dark plans she has up her proverbial sleeve. I narrow my eyes to convey her wickedness. Maybe she really is poor, the boy says, returning to his polishing. Does it matter? I ask, I don't care if she is one step away from a ditch, I won't make any jellies with her. If it is true that the house is rotting and she has to bring in some hags from town to cook up plum jellies to sell, they better not count on me to help. I don't know a jelly from a . . . I trail off. Blancmange? the boy says helpfully. Yes, I say, Blancmange. I can't cook and that's genetic. If they try to force me, something terrible could happen, something in me might burst, a valve to my heart or a nerve I need in my brain. But you can boil milk, the boy says, You used to boil milk for me when we lived in the city. That's true, I admit, I did boil milk and I did it well. And Mr. Marcolini, the boy adds, Remember, we made eggs for him those times? Hmm, I say because these things the boy says are absolutely true. It is quite likely that I am a great, or at least competent, cook. But I won't boil milk for the mother, I tell him, She can beg to kingdom come but I will never so much as heat a teaspoon for that slut. The boy leaves his sandals to dry and begins a series of rapid jumping jacks. It certainly wouldn't kill him to get a little exercise. If I can help it, I would rather not be associated with a fat child. There was no chance of the boy getting fat back in the Piazza Navona. In those days we were like greyhounds. Only slower, of course. Ten, eleven, twelve, the boy whispers, jumping. He is quite correct, back in the city I cooked more than a few breakfasts for our old landlord, though I may have killed him. I may have killed our landlord but not from food poisoning. If in fact I did kill Mr. Marcolini, it was from shouting while he rested, it was from awakening him with a violence for which he was ill prepared. We might never know what befell our landlord but one thing is certain: my cooking was not to blame. In fact, it is quite likely that my cooking provided the old man with the sweetest of his final moments here on earth. I may be a very good cook, I say, testing how the sentence sounds. After all, Mr. Marcolini always seemed very pleased by his breakfasts. The boy stops jumping. I made the toast, he says. Yes you did, I say, And you made it well. It is you and I who should be in business together cooking jellies and selling them, not the old crone downstairs. My memory of cooking is the look of distress which crossed my husband's face every evening

as he apprehended some green forked thing, his nervous side-
long looks as I stood triumphant with a brisket. In fairness I
cannot say that the dishes I served that sweet man who worshipped me were in any way tasty, though they may have been
nutritious. Edmund's brother starts jumping again, counting to
himself softly. That old husband of mine was as healthy a Bavarian as you could wish to meet, but he hated our suppers. Perhaps I have become a better cook over the years or perhaps I
cared for my landlord's pleasure more than that of my husband.
An interesting thing to chew on, this idea that I am an able, if
not excellent, cook. And if I am an excellent cook, one who is
simply missing the pie numbers, the case can be made that I am
not a hard woman at all. How dreadful that you can cook eggs
into your grave and still be named a hard woman at the ceme-
tery. The boy stops jumping and sits on the edge of the bed, out
of breath. Edmund said something else, I tell the boy. A look
passes over his face; he gets up from the bed and moves away
from me to stand against the wall, palms pressed flat against it.
It pains me to tell you this, I say, But Edmund said something
very disturbing a few moments ago. The boy sweeps some hair
from his face and I notice his hand is trembling. What on earth
is wrong with you this morning? I ask. Nothing, he says quickly.
What did Edmund tell you? Well, I say, smoothing the covers
again, This is difficult for me to repeat. I look up at the boy. He
said he loved me. The boy's shoulders sag. I know, I say, Very,
very odd. The boy walks to the window again. Why would he

say that? the boy asks. I push my feet out the bottom of the blankets to examine my toes. I have no idea, I say, But it disturbs me, I can tell you that much. The boy stares into the garden. We must resist love, he murmurs. I get out of bed, feeling the itch to pace. There are certain theories, certain postulates I have shared with you that I could never share with Edmund, I tell the boy. You must keep in mind that though you share a common lineage, you and Edmund have different sized brains. You know that I have committed myself to the resistance of love, I say, That only in resistance can we be free. We have spoken of it many times, you and I. Your brother, on the other hand, I say, I have never spoken to him of my theories. Edmund is mysterious to us, but he provides for us so we must take care never to malign him. I understand it is some sort of hell to live inside his head and this is why he turns his back to us over and over. Where you and I can contain many notions, including ideas that exist in direct opposition to one another, Edmund's brain is such that, in order to consider even the most mundane supposition, he must turn away from the world. We must never jump to conclusions about what it means to be Edmund. We must never assume that because Edmund does not face us he does not care for us. Clearly he cares for us. He might even love us, whatever love means. Certainly there were times in the beginning, I say. The boy slides down the wall. When he showed you the beetle? he says. That's right, I tell him, Exactly right. As you recall, it was one day not long after our meeting at the

Alpine Inn. We sat together watching skiers come in from their athletics. An insect of some kind had landed on the floor between us in a kind of huzzing dance. Is that a bee? a man next to us asked as he warmed himself in front of the fire. Wrong, the boy says, You're wrong, the man says he's allergic. I motion to bring me the cigarettes. Trust me, I say, That comes later. You see, first the man wanted to establish that he had something to worry about. Edmund's brother hands me the cigarettes and casts around for the matches. Over there, I tell him, pointing to the window ledge. Your brother told the man, No, it's a beetle. Well the man shakes his big head and says, My friend, unless I am very much mistaken, that is a bee; now will you please kill it? I look at Edmund's brother, Can you imagine? *Now,* I say, nodding my head to indicate this is where allergy fits into the story, The man tells Edmund, I happen to be *allergic.* Well you can picture your brother's reaction, I say, lighting up the cigarette. For all his faults, Edmund would never execute a living thing simply because he was given the order. Edmund got up and walked over to the bug. He picked it up and brought it to me, setting it on the armrest of my chair. We bent over it closely, checking that yes, yes, it owned the flat body and head of a beetle, not the cylindrical shape of the bee, which is a different species altogether. Edmund did not bother to lord his superior grasp of insects over the man; in effect he, well, he turned his back to him. At the window, the boy is wrapping his head in the curtain cord. Your brother and I sat very close together huddled over our small living friend whose life we had just spared, I continue. It was as if Edmund had presented me with something very rare and beautiful, this gift. For there was no reason to show it to me rather than the mustachioed stranger by his side. There was only one reason, I thought the next morning, as I lay in bed next to my traveling companion, unable to sleep. When you want to look at a person very closely sometimes you have to examine a third thing together; sometimes that is the best way to do it. This is what comes to mind when the word *love* is spoken, looking at a third thing. Eventually the stranger got to his feet and wandered away. But before he did he stopped in front of us and said, I am *allergic* to bees, *vous comprenez?* The boy puts his hand over his mouth and laughs; this is his favorite part of the story. *Vous comprenez?* he repeats, sniggering. The stranger had an extremely red nose; I think he was quite drunk. I suck on my cigarette. Yes, I murmur, He brought me a beetle. I have not thought of that beetle for some time.

The boy goes back to playing with the curtain cord, pretending to become asphyxiated. I have never told Edmund how ridiculous I find him, I remark, Perhaps I should. The boy opens one eye. Are you coming back from the dead? I ask. He nods. Do you think I should inform Edmund of my reservations, so he won't grow to loathe me? The boy shrugs. Perhaps things would be different, I say quietly, getting up to untangle the brother from his noose.

The boy breathes on the window and draws a face in the condensation. Dear God, I say, You know how it grieves me when you behave like a child. I find it immensely stressful. I put a hand to my heart. I have felt so embolic since arriving at the mother's. Don't be surprised if, when they cut me open, they find a massive thrombosis right about here, I say, palpating a spot on my chest. Tell them I had a feeling, I say. The boy nods, without concern I should mention. Without concern. Where is your green notebook? I ask. This is exactly the sort of thing that needs to be written down. How are you to remember without notes? The boy grins and taps his head. Marvelous, I tell him, Certainly I have no doubt. But where will our biographers be without any sort of papers to examine? The boy crosses to the night table and pulls open a drawer. It is vital to have *papers,* I remind him. While we would never want our history to be hagiographic, we must leave some tempting papers behind. I light a cigarette. As soon as I light it, I see my last, unfinished, smoldering on the window ledge. Where was I? I say, licking my finger to extinguish my new cigarette in order to finish the first. Ah yes, I say, giving the old cigarette a terrific suck, Everyone who survives us will want to tear us down. They will tell the most violent fibs about us; the only way we have a fighting chance is to leave behind some appealing papers. Out of the accidental and the trivial, our biographer will conjure a meaningful story. Though we might feel our lives meant nothing as we lived them, when we read our biography we will discover in fact we led great and meaningful lives. Yes, I murmur, We must hope not to die before we read it.

Edmund's brother takes out the green notebook from a drawer in his night table. What time is it? he asks. I look at the clock. Seven something, I say, Seven fifteen. You see what sort of start we have on the day? That's one nice thing about being damned, I suppose; it gets you up in the morning. Imagine, I say, Had it been an excellent morning we would still be lounging in bed. So that's good, I murmur, Lucky us to be so damned. The boy looks at me over the top of his green notebook. Where should we begin? I ask. Perhaps we should begin from the time you came to Edmund and me at the Piazza Navona; then we could work backward and forward simultaneously filling in odd bits of my life and any additional philosophies I care to disclose. Edmund's brother nods. On the other hand, I say, We could begin at my beginning. We look at each other, the boy and I; he with his head cocked to one side like a bird, me with my head straight on, like a person. This is how we communicate sometimes; silently, and I am usually smoking. If I am pacing and we wish to implement this silent communication, then I usually stop and turn and we share a thought in that manner. I take your point, I tell him, exhaling, And I think you are quite correct. Only an obvious person would begin at the beginning and we have struggled our entire lives to behave unpredictably. Here's a third idea, I say. Let's begin with a thunderclap moment. After all, we are not writing our biography; we are simply leaving papers, or notations, scrapings in the sand, am I right? The boy nods. In which case, we can begin with anything and leave it up to our biographer to make sense of it. It's not our job to connect the blessed dots. Why not begin with a thrilling tale, something relentless that will lure a potential biographer? The boy shakes his pen to encourage ink flow. Maybe some day a man will be going through our things, he says, And he wasn't even going to write a book until he found our papers. Yes, yes, I say but the thought of a stranger elbow-deep in my private treasures suddenly unnerves me. I think we will leave our papers in a prominent place when we feel the time is right, I tell the boy. When we are about to die? he asks. Yes, I confirm, When we feel we might be dying we will set out our papers so our biographer need not rifle through our personal items. I am staring at the mother's vile carpet, hypnotized by its pattern of cabbage roses trailing around the perimeter, trying to find my way back into the story. I have completely lost my place. So the thunderclap moment, the boy says, Is the thunderclap moment when we were archivists? No, I tell him firmly, That was never anything. I take a deep suck on my cigarette. I will never think about that time, on account of its troubling conclusion. Well what about your history prize? the boy asks. My foot creeps across the carpet to amend some fallen ash. The history prize, I murmur. I stare at the end of my cigarette, ostensibly to provide no more ash dives off its end but in fact an awful dread is advancing through me. In the light of my hypothetical biography I am forced to face that my life's crowning achievement might boil down to the history prize I won at the age of thirteen. Veterans of war might feel the same on their deathbed. The prize, the honor, the glory, how it all amounts to nothing in the end. Out in the garden a woodpecker molests a tree; the noise ricochets up to us. Clearly the history prize is the last of my validations; I have sought to annihilate each one. I excel at this, this remorseless assassination, a defrocking of sorts. I have nothing. But there is the boy. I have Edmund's brother and one day he will march into the world and do very brave and important things. And I will be there somewhere, if not with him, then within him.

Mama? the boy says. I look at him over my cigarette. What will we start with? the boy asks again, What is the thunderclap to put in our papers? I don't know, I say, I am still thinking. Give me a moment, I say. Surely there have been many important thunderclap moments suitable for beginning a biography. I think my days at the bank were never dramatic, I say slowly. The boy shakes his head. Not the bank, he says, No one wants to read about some old bank. I stretch out my feet and cross them at the ankle. Then I recross them the other way. My feet please me enormously today. Often on a day like today, when I have woken to damnation or when we have been struck by a

particularly violent expression of weather, I will find something
new that gratifies me, usually some long-suffering part of my
body that deserves noticing. Today it is my feet. I have never
appreciated the sleek diagonal of my toes. Some day I will run
out of new things to like about myself. Yet there will always be
hats to crave. I like the sound of this last and say it aloud,
repeating it several times but altering the quality of my voice
each time. Should I write that down? the boy asks, Because a
hat isn't much of a thunderclap. I walk over to the window
ledge. Where is my new cigarette, the one I purposefully extin-
guished in order to save? I ask. The boy points toward the night
table with his pen. I don't think you are in charge of my thunderclap, I tell him as I go to the night table, At the same time I
believe you are correct; a hat is no thunderclap. I am in no
mood to lecture on metaphor. I light the cigarette for the second time and regard the boy. He is busy macerating something
in his mouth. What on earth have you got in there? I ask. He
opens his mouth to extract a dingy white ball. Paper, he says politely. I cross my arm and support it with the opposite elbow. I
am giving him the old up and down look that on a better day
would have us in hysterics. What am I to do with you? I ask. I
buy you the best notebook in Rome in order that you have a
home for my wisdom and you proceed to eat the damn thing.
He giggles but removes the remaining paper from his mouth. I
have no thunderclap, I say finally. I have walked to the window
then back to the bed and even to the very lintel of the door, all

to no avail. There is no grand entrance to my life, no life-changing moment. I look over at Edmund's brother. He is staring at the clock on his night table. What time is it now? he asks. I look at the clock, then back at him. You've never shown any sort of interest in time before, I say. Have you been reading something? He shakes his head. Well it's half past the seven, I tell him. I think we might begin with some other event in the hope that our biographer will be a patient man or that along the way we will happen upon my thunderclap moment. Leave the first page blank, I instruct. Edmund's brother makes a great fuss of turning the page, licking his pen and looking at me with great expectation. Sometimes I worry about the old husband I left behind, I say importantly, given to the biographical turn. He was forgetful about eating, sleeping as well. Sometimes as I lay beside him unable to sleep I wondered whether he had perhaps installed me in his compound as a witness. I would like to be the woman to say I was planted there to care for him, that I remain to make certain he ate well and attended mass. But I am not that woman. Perhaps Samina is that woman, I have no way of knowing, but as I stand here today I worry about my dear husband who never asked that much from me. I look at the boy. Write this down, I say, I would like my husband to know that once upon a time this woman had more on her mind than the rats in his pool, that though she may not have *appeared* to care, in fact she cared very much. Or at least a medium amount, I amend. If Samina has not replaced me in my husband's compound he might well have starved to death, I say. I may not have cooked the most pleasant meals for that man, but they were meals and I am unsure whether, left to his own devices, my husband would know how to operate any of the cooking equipment. I hope he has not gassed himself, I say, turning to the boy. What if he has accidentally gassed himself? That would make me feel horrible. Our stove had no automatic pilot. My husband may have waited so long for the flame that he grew woozy and succumbed to the mortal effects of gas. I do not like to think of the police stumbling on my husband draped across the kitchen floor clad in nothing but his thermals. That would be a ghastly way to go, I say. Perhaps I should have left instructions detailing how to use the stove. My husband never liked the police in our town, he found them gossipy and discourteous. It would pain him greatly to be found wearing his thermals, which bore a delicate pattern of snowflakes around the waist and terminals. My husband imagined no one but me would ever chance to see the snowflakes on his thermals; to be found dead and clad in them, by such discourteous men as the town police—it's unbearable to think about. I pace, agitated. On the other hand, it is equally likely that my husband quickly came to realize that our gas requires a match to ignite and set about making his eggs Florentine with dispatch. If my husband is still living, it is probable that Samina is standing exactly where I once stood, lighting the gas for all his meals and turning meat in the pan once it had browned on one side. And if Samina has supplanted me in the affections of my husband, it only stands to reason that she has also bought the love of my cat. If my old husband returned to my bank to secure a new wife for his compound that woman, perhaps Samina, perhaps another, would instantly try to buy her way into the affections of my cat, I tell Edmund's brother. The boy shifts in his chair. Are these part of your papers? he asks. Am I supposed to be writing this down? I think for a minute, pulling a piece of tobacco off my tongue. No, I say thoughtfully, I think this is more of an aside; this is more something I am telling you to flesh out the portrait of Samina. I can't think this will be of any interest to some potential biographer who finds my papers and God knows we don't need to give Samina any share of the limelight. The boy nods. There is a good chance my old moggy will prove faithful and give the new wife a deep scratch or two, but there's an equally likely chance that my cat was quite glad to see the back of me that day I stole into the night. Perhaps I only appear in the nightmares of my cat, I add. And perhaps I appear to her then as a looming shadowy presence that once fed her to the point of bursting, who can say. Under Samina's care she might now hover close to the weight of a regular cat, there is no way to know. No way to tell. The moral here, I say pointedly, nodding toward the green notebook, Write this down. Is that the love we give is not necessarily the same love received; something happens over the transom. Yes, I murmur, Over the transom. I stare into the middle distance of the bedroom considering whether this is very wise or simply common sense. Or indeed, utterly fatuous.

As I turn back to the window to begin a new thought I catch the boy staring at something past my shoulder. I follow his gaze; it stops at the clock. I swivel my head back to the boy. He is absorbed in the examination of his index finger; he appears to be flaying the tip of it. That's a little too innocent, my friend, I say darkly. The boy picks up his pen and looks at me with artificial interest. What comes next? he asks. Edmund's brother is becoming just like Sally. All show. *What comes next*, as if I have not one second ago caught him ogling the clock. Unfortunately I have found that to address the obsession is only to prolong the obsession. How many times when we lived on the Piazza Navona did the boy suddenly become obsessed with one thing over all others. There was, for example, the time of the birds. For weeks we were unable to leave the house without carrying with us an immense book showing the different profiles of starlings and robins and blue jays. The boy was besotted with the birds. If I succeeded in leaving without the book he would remember it before we had crossed the street and insist on doubling back for it. Everywhere we went the boy was tripping over his feet as he turned his head again and again to the Roman sky hoping to identify a bird other than the filthy pigeons that flew there. Next, an indiscriminate fixation with any machine devoted to road repair. During that miserable phase every turn in the road seemed to offer a new vista of yellow cranes and diggers all ripe for identifying. And now: the clock. Soon enough we will learn the waltz of big and little hands and how they come to tell us what they know, I tell the boy. But is it half past eight? he asks. No, I say, Not yet. What happens at half past eight, you have to give your shoes a second polish? I ask. The boy glances at his sandals waiting on their sheet of newspaper and shakes his head. No sandals today, I tell him. We are going out into the fields and for that we require tall boots such as Wellingtons. If the gardener has fixed our net as Edmund promises, then we will spend a good part of our day collecting specimens in the field, I tell him. I would not like to see those fine shoes of yours get muddied after you have spent so many minutes caring for them. The boy says nothing. Go get washed, I say. I am bored of my biography. There is more to life than biography.

Edmund's brother walks across the room and disappears into the washroom. He is growing older, becoming a man. The boy no longer needs me to carry him to and fro. He is quite able to get to the washroom on his own; if not to make the decision, at least to carry it out. I fall into bed. This morning, after the brother has finished his washing and brushing and has dressed in his eight-year-old clothes, we will venture into the greenery outside the mother's house with our magnifying glass, several jars for housing specimens and perhaps the butterfly net if the indolent gardener has finally mended it. Much later in one of

the cool dark rooms on the second floor we will gaze at our vic-
tims and tell their biographies to each other in little insect
voices. Unlike his brother, the boy will illustrate his ready wit.
The boy will show me the agility of his brain; a thing Edmund
has never done. It is very likely that Edmund's brother will win
prizes in school one day. With my guidance and instruction the
boy will grow to do many intelligent and interesting things. I
may lie in bed for the rest of my life, I may be obliterated by Edmund's stupidity, but the boy will march out into this great
wide world and make something of himself. Perhaps one day
when I am old and it pains my joints to climb excessive stairs,
Edmund's brother will return to hold my hand and ease my pain
and recount his thrilling tales. I will make us tea; I will offer biscuits I save especially for his visits. At some point I will shuffle
across the kitchen and with great pride hold up the potholder
I've spent my hours knotting from discarded string. Yes, while
the boy grows more and more agitated from the close air and
smell of dying I will cluck and gasp and show him the thousands of useless domestic objects I have spent my final hours
assembling. That will be my summation. My aunt had her many
memories to accompany her as she lay dying of emphysema. No
doubt she relived her days flying around the Italian countryside
in borrowed cars or feeding elephants in India. I have seen the
photographs; I heard her stories. If I were to die today I have
not nearly enough memories to comfort me during a lingering
death. If I am crippled suddenly with a bizarre disease, one that

propels my doctors to a reference library, I may have enough memories to accompany those final moments. Otherwise I will be forced to repeat memories. On the other hand, perhaps I will be given a television. Watching television on my deathbed would certainly require fewer lifetime memories. I could watch television right up to my final hour, then quickly snap it off and trot out my scant memories for my journey to the beyond. As I consider this I am suddenly aware that my eyeballs are flicking painfully back and forth in my head. I close my eyes. Alas it is quite impossible to predict the exact moment of expiration. It would be troubling to find one has spent one's life avoiding the pollution of television only to end up dying with some musical comedy blaring in the background. On the other hand, since you would be dead, you wouldn't know. But those gathered around your bed would have a good chortle. And at your expense, too. I hear the door to the bathroom open. Do you know, I say to the boy without opening my eyes, It strikes me I have always placed death in this special place; a place that caps everything I have known, the very worst of places where in fact perhaps death is the best of places, a place to arrive at, the place where everything begins. I open my eyes. Edmund's brother is freshly scrubbed, his hair slicked down. Thank God you have attended to your hair, I say, pulling back the bedcovers, I did not like to mention it but you were beginning to take on certain characteristics of our old friend Toby. The boy picks up his sandals from the newspaper. You haven't forgotten Toby? I say, pinching my nose. No, he says quietly, I remember. Toby was a stinker, he says. Well that's putting it mildly, I say. You know I feel quite refreshed after lying down for a few minutes, I say. And while it is true that I have been considering my own horrible end, for whatever reason thoughts of my death have cheered me immensely and even given me a bit of an appetite. I almost feel like whistling, I tell Edmund's brother. The brother, more than anyone, knows that I never whistle. For me to want to whistle means this day has had a real turnaround. From my initial damnation to now, there's been a real revolution. I am not certain why thoughts of my own suffering have turned the day around but sometimes it is unwise to examine things too closely. I am so intent on thoughts of our future—my dying one, the boy's quite bright one—that it is only after I have followed Edmund's brother downstairs that I notice a number of unusual details. *Primo:* we have come to rest in the parlor. No one uses the mother's parlor, ever. *Secondo:* the boy is wearing short trousers and a fresh white shirt. The boy never wears short trousers on account of his acute sensitivity to the cold. Sometimes in the Piazza Navona we would fall back in bed soon after rising, that's how sharply we both feel the cold. Yes, we always freeze, the boy and I, especially at the equinox. Exactly like me, the boy finds chills gather at the neck. We both require mufflers for this reason. And neither of us ever wears short trousers specifically for this reason. In each hand Edmund's brother holds his sandals, the pair I bought for him one day in Rome, back when it was just the two of us. I stand in the parlor doorway regarding the unfamiliar room. What a dead room this is, I say, What on earth are we doing here? Edmund's brother bends and places his sandals on the floor next to his feet. Look at you, I say. You'll freeze to death in those short trousers, I say, Is that what you're hoping for? The boy ignores me. Where did you come across those ridiculous things, anyway? The boy forces one foot, then the next into his sandals, then bends to buckle them. You know, I find this ignoring of yours to be terribly boring, I say, lighting a cigarette. Others may find it inventive but it bores me to pieces. If you are angry I imagine you could come up with a more original means of expressing it after all the time I invest in teaching you to be singular. The boy finishes buckling his shoes and turns around. I face him, one arm supporting my elbow as I smoke. I raise my eyebrows. The boy pushes his feet deeper into his sandals. He gazes at the floor, gathering his courage. Then he looks up at me, suddenly emboldened, a new glint in his eye. Edmund was supposed to tell you, he says. I puff on the cigarette. Tell me? I say, Tell me what? Edmund told me several things, each more insane than the one before. The boy presses his mouth into a thin line and I suddenly see the resemblance to Edmund, the pale disapproval. I knew it, the boy says bitterly. Tell me what? I say, Somebody tell me, whatever it is! Fine, he says, I'll tell you. He sighs. I am dressed like this, the boy says, Because I am going to school. Silence. Today, he adds.

The only sound is the sizzle of my cigarette as it burns. From far away, upstairs perhaps, the sound of running water starts. I shake my head as if to loosen something. What? You are doing *what*, exactly? Edmund's brother looks up at me, his little face screwed up like a fist. I am going to school, he says again. So here it is, my damnation, not a dream after all. Edmund's brother and I stare at each other through smoke. His look is one of defiance; he stands braced as if against a strong wind. Well, I say finally, Since you are going to *schooool* may I suggest you zip up your trousers? Unless of course this school requires its boys to expose themselves. Unzipped trousers may be this school's orthodoxy, I have no way of knowing. I find I have lost the taste for my cigarette. A large flower arrangement stands next to the fireplace. I walk to it and dispose of my cigarette. Air rushes by my ears as if I am falling from a great height. It takes me a year to reach the urn; I watch the clock on the mantel tick minutes as I walk. It is nearly nine, a time when children the world over gather in chalky rooms ready to nod in acquiescence to teachers who know less than nothing. All those heads nodding together, pulled by a common string. Finally I reach the flowers; I stub out the cigarette and drop it in the vase. I turn to the boy, who has untucked his shirt in order to retuck it. My, I say, How fastidious we are today. The boy continues with his shirt. Here's what I find interesting, I say,

walking to the window and looking out, Perhaps you can en-
lighten me. Did you *tell* someone you wanted to go to school? I
say, turning. Did you mention something to that horrible
woman with dead eyes? I am struggling to keep my voice in
control when I very much want to shout. On the other hand,
the strain of keeping my voice at a normal level is creating some
sort of growl at the back of my throat that feels increasingly un-
pleasant. I am simply curious, I say with a smile. Merely interested. Who had this idea? This *school* idea? The back of my
throat feels thick with pain. I went to school when I lived with
my mum and dad, he whispers. Yes, I say, Yes, we know that already. Every time I turn around you're chattering on about this
magical time with your mum and dad, I say. Anyone would
think to hear you speak of it that you and I had never had any
sort of special time together. Any stranger listening to you harp
on about your mum and blessed dad would think that a stranger
who boiled your milk for nearly a year on the Piazza Navona
had done nothing more than inconvenience you on your route
to school. I turn back to the window and attempt to force it
open. Did I or did I not teach you things? I ask, quickly abandoning the effort. Did I not sacrifice my own ambitions in order to ensure you do not grow into a stupid man? I drop my
voice and point to where we could see Edmund if there were no
walls between us. Your brother, I tell the boy, Will never know
the benefit of my wisdom. He simply does not possess the
means to synthesize it. Do you want to become that person? I

ask the boy. Is that the man you wish to grow into, stupid and beautiful? Because let me tell you, son, I say without knowing exactly why I have called the boy *son,* Let me tell you, I continue, I know what those schools do and it is not pretty. I feel calmer and I take out a cigarette. No sir, I say, lighting a match. In fact there is no sight more disturbing than that of a boy sitting in a classroom as his mind drains away, as his imagination is forced to align with the imaginations of the very average children sitting next to him on either side. There was one thing I always hoped you would take from our times in Rome, one thing, I say. Do you recall what it was? The boy looks to the heavens. Oh, that ceiling won't help you, I say. He sighs. Come on, I say, You remember the one thing, don't you, the one thing? I feel like I am begging, I must look like my old cat pleading for sustenance. Well, I finally say, Perhaps I failed, then. Perhaps you are quite right to go to school after all. There was only one thing? he asks. *Nooo,* I say. Clearly I taught you more than *one* thing but the most important thing. Never listen to other people? he says. Exactly! I say louder than I planned. That's exactly right. I taught you to listen only to— *You,* the boy says, interrupting me. I fan the smoke away to find him. No, I say slowly, The lesson I was teaching was to trust your instincts. Once you gathered some, that is; until then my instincts were good enough. The boy says nothing. We hear Edmund's mother calling the boy's name. We stare at each other not moving as we hear footsteps on the stairs, as we hear the door to the parlor open, as the dead-eyed mother enters to take the boy away. What about your hot milk? I ask, Are you planning to go to school with nothing in your stomach? They both look at me blankly. I turn away and walk back to the stubborn window. And your blazer? I ask, looking out to the garden, where an early frost has left the rosebushes silvery. The mother laughs. Her laughter comes like an old grievance, a thousand years old it is and full of decay. Blazer? she says, That Frankenstein job? I threw it in the dustbin. Edmund's mother learned English from the television, which renders her nearly impossible to understand. And gets my back up, if you will. The boy should have a blazer for school, I say firmly. That much is evident, no boy should go to school on his first day without one. I turn around; that way I see the mother holding up a grey blazer, schoolboy size, over her arm. I see, I say. So this has all been planned for some time, I say, This *school* business. It seems the entire household was in on the plan. For weeks everyone has been skulking around the house whispering behind their palms and enjoying themselves enormously at my expense. And while you have all been engaged in your amateur theatrics, I have been continuing my studies with the boy. Everyone, I say, Running around, purchasing blazers, *lying* to me. What sort of lesson is that for the boy? *Lying* to me? Did the gardener know? I ask bitterly. Did the deceit extend to every part of the household? And does this have something to do with the disappearance of my butterfly net? I ask. Because it once belonged to my father. I look at the floor, as I like to do when I need some control. That net is personal property, I whisper, And I will not have it destroyed in the name of your fun. I am barefoot and even my feet, which pleased me such a short time ago, now aggravate me beyond measure. I curl my toes under. Well, the mother says in a meaningful tone. I look up. The two of them stand close together, as if they guard something. Has the school been informed about tomatoes? I ask. Because they should know. If someone tries to feed the boy tomatoes, or anything red for that matter, he will fly into a rage. There will be no pacifying him if tomatoes find their way onto his plate, I say. They both look at me silently, quizzically. I turn back to the window. Well go then, I say. I can hear the boy reach up to take the mother's hand; I know the sound of that sleeve only too well. When a man holds out a cucumber sandwich on white bread, somewhere in the back of his head he is plotting your downfall. Yes, behind his back he holds a great sharp knife.

I walk to the front door to watch the mother and the boy drift down the long drive toward the village. I stand in the doorway watching as they grow smaller and smaller until I can no longer see them. Then I close the door. I slump against the wall and find myself quickly entangled in coats and scarves that hang there on a series of hooks. Even the sight of the mother's hat, which I have longed to wear since my arrival, cannot brighten my mood. It takes several minutes to find my way out of the coats and scarves. They have taken him from me, I say aloud, repeating it many times in the empty hall. I want to lie on the floor face down with my nose pressed against the carpet. The house is terribly quiet, eerily so. My heart seems to beat in my ears. I wander into the kitchen. The ticking of the clock soon drives me out. I spend several minutes watching two ants try to carry a humongous crumb; I notice these workers are headed toward the window ledge and help them over on a piece of cardboard I rip from a box. The gardener passes a window carrying a pitchfork and I watch him vigilantly, hoping he might trip, perhaps impale a limb. In a bookcase in the living room I find what I am looking for; I noticed it there when we first arrived. I slide out the mother's leather-bound copy of *Moby Dick,* caressing it like a treasure I have found after a brutal search that lasted many years and left me with fewer digits. So, I whisper, Here we are again, whale. But I find I cannot open the cover. A tempest rages in my head; I cannot contain the image of the boy trotting off to school with his empty stomach. As I consider the heavy book in my hand, I chance to look out the window. Edmund has not moved from his spot before the tree. I throw the book on a chair, snatch my coat and race outside fuelled by a sudden burst of rage. A rage so intense I can scarcely get my arms into the sleeves of my coat.

I storm up to Edmund. You love me? I say. What was that supposed to mean: you *love* me? Edmund takes a step back. You

lacked the courage to tell me the boy was being taken to
school? I ask. He shrugs. I'm a coward, he says. Oh, far more
than that, I say. You, I search for the word, You, sir, are a—*Judas.*
And without waiting for an answer I march away, across the
lawn toward the wood that abuts it. He loves me, *really.* What
does he take me for? I slow down at the bottom of the hill, once
I have disappeared from Edmund's sight.

When we first came to this cold place I took the boy outside one night so I could point to the stars. We lay on a blanket
I had taken from the mother's bed and brought outside for
our comfort. Don't be awed by stars, I told him as we made
ourselves comfortable. Are the constellations magnificent? I
asked. They certainly are. And there is certainly every reason to
appreciate the night sky. But, in looking up, I ask that you
never feel your finite shell. I ask that you never feel small and
mortal or insignificant. Yes, we are staring at billions of years of
unexplained collisions and the great unfolding universe. But
your troubles are still of consequence. Don't tuck yourself away
in a corner because life is too huge. Remember, no star has ever
built a road. And I guarantee you no star ever wrote a beautiful
book about a whale, I said. We sat up so the boy could light my
cigarette. I have no idea why everyone is so desperate to feel
unimportant when it feels so good to be essential, I murmured
as the boy struck match after match. We lay down again and my
cigarette burned in the darkness, our private star. That was a
good night.

As I cross away from Edmund I shove my hands deep into the pockets of my coat. My fingers close around the soccer photograph I have kept on my person for so long. Without a second thought I draw out the photograph, look at it one final time then rip it to pieces and let them fall. There's to your bloodless coup. I am still walking as I tear the picture so I have to double back and pick up a few bigger pieces to shred them further. Then I gallop away from the house until my lungs scream from the fresh air. Slow down, I think. A few deep breaths. I don't care to encounter a heart problem right now. At the edge of the lawn a narrow path breaks into a birch-lined lane. Other trees blend into each other entangling limbs and leaves, reluctant to give their names; not the birch. White bark, black branch, the birch. As I lose sight of the house, I take more deep breaths. I need to calm down. I try to recall breathing exercises taught to prevent hyperventilation but I cannot remember which are the exercises and which are examples of the affliction. It could be that, in trying to thwart hyperventilation, I am encouraging it instead. Sometimes, in order to calm me, perhaps when Samina was working my nerves or an office machine had broken down, my bank manager, Mr. Harper, used to raise his hand to shoulder height and, palm down, slowly lower it. I would become hypnotized by his slowly lowered hand and immediately grow calmer. I lean my head back to take in the sky, the color of pigeon, and think of the pencil sharpener Mr. Harper had affixed to his wall. Thoughts of the sharpener, its humble function, have been a tonic in uncertain times. Depressing a small lever allowed a dial to be rotated that in turn allowed the correctly sized pencil-hole to line up with another hole granting access to the blade. As the person charged with sharpening pencils every morning, I always rotated this dial back then forth in order to locate the hole of the correct size, though the girth of our pencils never changed. It seemed imperative to honor the adaptability of the machine even if only one hole was exploited over and over. As much as I loved depressing the lever and turning the dial, what I loved most of all was operating the crank. Perhaps the boy's new school will have such a device. He will love operating the crank as well as I once did. Several clouds move to the northeast, that is what I take to be the northeast; it may very well be the southwest. They suggest rain in the afternoon. Beyond the lane, less trodden paths snake into the woods, creating alluring spaces between the trees. Alluring to some, I mean, for they never tempt me. Bears, newts, frogs, these are no friends of mine though I like to gaze into the green and brown tangle from the safety of the lane. I like to know there is a wilderness but I do not wish to know it well. I have no interest in facing a bear or cougar and have to quickly sift my memory for the correct response, be it to run or climb a tree or cast myself face down and mime death. The thought of miming death, muddying myself, keeps me away from nature most of the time. From the lane I can gaze with serenity at roots and mud and greenery. There are times when I have stepped off the path to stir a few pebbles with the toe of my boot or examine a fern, but I never delve any further than that. I use nature like the slut she is; from a safe distance I find my thoughts in some rock or swamp, then I quickly retreat. I cannot bear to think for more than a minute on the boy's little pink face, one among many little pink faces. If his teacher assumes that the best way to educate the boy is to give him rows of words to memorize, he has chosen the wrong child. Had anyone asked me, I would have prepared a manifesto suggesting the best approach. Edmund's brother is a very stubborn boy with the likelihood of serious learning problems down the road. It would behoove them not to make the mistake of treating the boy like a normal child. I step off the lane into a small wooded grove a short distance from the road. A dry log makes an excellent spot to sit and think. I have been here before. The mother does not like me to smoke but in this grove I sometimes light a cigarette and think back to a time when there was no mother, when it was just the three of us in our beloved rooms on the Piazza Navona. But I have no intention of thinking about Edmund or his brother at this time. Right now I need to consider my future. I am in a grove, a place to dwell on crossroads, thresholds or turning points. I lean against a birch to assess the house and grounds and the earth at my feet and the bits of shrubs and ferns and green things around me, weeds perhaps or herbs, vegetal matter that an innovative person could live on for weeks but which would kill me within the hour. If forced to camp, which I pray may never come to pass, I am certain to happily ingest poisonous plants while those about me feast correctly. The sun brightens the sky, the kind of late October sun that plies the mother's lawns with a golden light. I am not a declarer of beauty and there is no one in my grove to whom I might declare it were I that fool, but I feel a pang. The nondeclarers, we silent types, feel it too. The words *golden light* appear in my mind as determined by the sun's rising. Exactly like that, *golden* followed by *light*. Nothing more inventive than that. Painful to hear in my head the words I associate with mangled descriptions of our sun, rising or setting or simply hanging above a beach somewhere tropical. *Golden light*. I have no choice, still I stare at the sun's colors and like them, heaven help me. While there is no declarer of beauty here to iterate the obvious, it seems I am a declarer too. Just as irritating, only silent. To all but me. The voice inside my head is a declarer of beauty whether I like it or not. And after all my hard work. Yet as much as I rail against the obviousness of innovation, a stirring in me wonders if I might be a poet. Poetry. A vocation I could still pursue, yes, yes with a little time and a good ink pen. I place my palm against the rough bark of an anonymous tree. How soothing rough textures can be to a distressed soul. The difficulty is that I cannot bear to read poetry. That is, I cannot bear to find sustenance where so many have found it before. And if I am to be a poet it will mean feeling things, which I would rather not; it will mean pimping each one of these *feelings* to the page. It seems a gruesome life to be struck mute by every trifle, as it seems the poets are. Poor little poets, harassing their tiny brains for new images. Out here in my grove these thoughts seem worthy of notation. Once upon a time I would have brought Edmund's brother with me, along with a ruler and his green notebook; together we would have unraveled these mysteries, helped along by ruled lines and ink. It occurs to me now that my lessons were also a form of pimping. I never owned my thoughts but, exactly like some poet, I found another use for them. Whenever I was struck by an ingenious idea I immediately began to formulate it for the benefit of Edmund's brother. Anxiously, I begin to plait my hair, quickly forming two braids that stick out, one over each ear. This affects a vise-like feeling to trap thoughts, one even more effective than the traditional ponytail. It is quickly clear that my life, my choices, do not belong to me and never have. From Daddy and Sally to my work at the bank and meeting Edmund, my entire life has been preordained by some bastard not me. My heart feels odd. I light another cigarette. I am not entirely certain where my first cigarette has ended up and I resolve to stay in the grove for several minutes to make sure a fire doesn't break out on the mother's property. I'm responsible like that, I may start the fire but I always stick around to extinguish it. Unless it's a real blaze; then I run like hell. The girl who scraped designs in the dirt with a thing she took for a stick but was in fact a dead man's finger, the girl who mistakenly brought her dying aunt grapes with seeds that promised to lodge in her raspy throat, does she despise me for bringing her to this place? Yes, in fact. How she hates me, my young self. And when I stand outside myself, which I admit is more often than not, it is with her eyes I see myself. It is her voice keeping me up all nights whispering You fucked up. And yet because she is gifted she curses me in French, which I have never understood. *Salope, putain, connasse.* I do not understand the brat because I have not lived up to her potential. Her invectives are lost on me. It is the eyes, to be frank, and I do the best I can, sir, it is the flinty eyes and sour breath, like a changeling at me day and night. Who could sleep with this specter hanging over me, this incubus I cannot shift? I hate to blame others for my lack of consequence, but I see no other choice. Who the hell was Daddy to force his notions of Sally and her pony on me almost from day one? Wet from the womb and Daddy waving Sally's life in front of my dim eyes, suggesting I behave exactly like this nubile maid with her tiresome pony. And before I was clever enough to burn the book, I sucked in a substantial amount of damaging information about the ways a girl needs to behave. Girls, the book suggested, Sit with Hands Clasped and Knees Together. And though it was not long before I was out in the park, sandwich tossed aside, head thrown to the sun, knees very much not together, the picture of dainty Sally had already been imprinted on my brain so that my entire life thus far has been a series of daily rebukes for not keeping Knees Together metaphorically or otherwise. Little Sally, aided by my father, well, their assault was systematic and pervasive. To this day I dream of Sally's shiny hair and know that I am less than Sally. You should applaud my genius that Sally was thrown into the fire when she was. Yes, yes not a moment too soon. There is no one to blame that I have no influence, no one but myself. However if someone were to ask in a conversational way whether one figure or another had negatively influenced my life, I might point a finger, not an accusing finger mind you, more of a helpful finger, in the direction of my bank manager. Mr. Harper attempted to squash me from my first day at his bank, a day when I arrived dressed exactly as little Sally might have dressed had the brat ever been forced to grow up and leave home. Had Sally ever had to leave the pages of her privileged life of horses and Mummy in order to contend with such things as rooming houses or wage packets, she might have worn the dress I chose for my first day at the bank. The dress was a wash of colors that suggested sunset. How could I not think of a way to lighten the morose hours that stretch after lunch? I chose that dress because it was a contrast to the browns and greys my customers wore, without being in any way the sort of harlot dress that can so easily cheapen a place like a bank. From my first day I thought of my customers. But the minute I set foot inside the bank, my manager, Mr. Harper, pulled me aside. Sunset hues were unwelcome in this particular bank, he said. In his bank there would be dresses in the duller end of the spectrum only. I did not hold this command against

Mr. Harper in any way but it bored me to take my orders from a man with such a limited imagination. There were so many other irksome rules; he had a little book of them. It was not a picture book like Sally's but it was still very clear. A mind of my own would not be tolerated. Of course my husband found me at the bank and for that I will always be surprised if not grateful. Certainly Samina is grateful as she sits beside him now worrying about the size and clarity of his alcohol, but I was never grateful. Those days I watched the rats caper in the dry pool or curiously lifted my head toward the distant sounds of church bells, never was I grateful I no longer worked in a bank. I never feel saved and that is my burden. Samina will feel saved as she stands in front of the steaming oven, salvaged from a life of deposits and withdrawals. With my old husband, I only felt that I was somewhere that was not a bank. Which is more of a fact than an emotion.

The grove is somewhat small for a good pace, the sort of pace I need given the morning's trials. This day has been a trial, my mother used to say. As a child I could never tell how the day being named a trial had differed from the one before. Now I understand. Little things mean to kill you. For my dear dead mother something as simple as the milk being off or running out of powder for the washing machine was enough to have the day be considered a *trial*. Of course sour milk could never compare to today, my day, this trial. My greatest wish at this instant is that this day might begin all over. If I could wake up for a second time and find I am not damned, that would please me enormously.

Hey. I look up. Edmund stands between two trees at the edge of the grove. I hold up my hand in salutation, then scramble to my feet because I cannot bear to be lower than him. May I join you? he says, coming forward. It makes me uneasy when Edmund uses correct English but I make room for him. Of course, I say, After all, it belongs to your mother. Edmund laughs. Don't laugh, I say, Don't laugh now, come on. Edmund comes forward pulling a bit of leaf off a tree and putting it in his mouth. We're country people now, he says, sitting down and pulling me down next to him. You may be, I say, But me? Never. The day I am a country person you have my permission to . . . Edmund looks at me. Permission to what? he asks. I shrug. I'm half dead anyway, I tell him. Edmund takes the leaf out of his mouth and regards it. I'm sorry, he says, It wasn't my idea. I thought you were doing a fine job. The boy seemed happy. He was happy, I say, You see. Did you tell your mother that? I did, he says, Of course I did. I lie back on the ground. Why did we come here? I say, Why did you bring us to this ossuary? Edmund leans over me; his entire body tips over mine. I missed you, he says. I put my hand on his chest. You must be a masochist, I tell him. He is very close; he smells like pine, one of the few smells I can tolerate. Come on, now, he says, Come on. Edmund begins to unplait my hair, shaking it free. As much as I tried to leave you behind I found myself remembering the commotion of your hair and those mad shoes that only a mad woman would wear. I put my hand on his shoulder. I am not mad, I say, Please don't call me that. I have been called mad my entire life and I am very, very bored of being called mad simply for the reason that I cannot abide the things that most abide. Edmund strokes my face, up from the chin, down from the hairline, breathing those irregular steady breaths of his from his enormous head. It happens that I become very, very calm when I am stroked in this manner. I am not mad, I say quietly. He takes his hand into my hair. But you are not normal, he says. I look into Edmund's eyes. Now there's a word I've never understood, I say. And I look past him up at the sky through the tree branches. I may have been ordinary once. October will turn to November and so forth. You left us alone in Rome, I say. Edmund touches the hollow at the base of my throat. Yes, he says, I had to define myself. I cough; I cannot bear to have my throat touched. And for that we had to starve? I say, For your definition we had to skulk about like dogs? Edmund laughs, he is full of laughter today. Come on, now, he says. What does it matter, we're all together again. Edmund stays, twirling my hair between two fingers, murmuring words that have no meaning. I think about the little boy sitting in his row among boys and girls who look exactly alike, only the girls will have longer hair and skirts. He will raise his hand when the smiling *professore* takes off his spectacles to posit a question about geography or the forest plants. We have learned so much together, the boy and I; he will know enough to indicate a need for the toilet; never again will he jig like he did in Rome. At the specified time all the boys and girls will rush into the playground in a lunatic swarm. There will be games, games involving hoops and bats and scores of all sorts. I trust he will not become impatient when he loses as, given the odds, he most certainly will at some point. In Rome we would have spent this day speeding around the city fuelled on the good coffee of our friend Toby. At length Edmund takes my hand and we walk back to the mother's house like lovers in some romance. The lamia has returned from her sad errand and now stands, legs akimbo, in her kingdom, assaulting items in the sink, one by one. She scarcely flinches when we pass the doorway. Edmund doubles back to ask what time the local school sets its captives free. Half past two, she tells him. In the corridor I point to Edmund's chest, spattered with paint. But he is cupping my face in his palms, kissing me, not caring about his chest and its paint. Now we are us again, he says, Just us two, as it was before my brother came to Rome. Yes, I murmur as if that is a good thing.

Edmund pulls me upstairs to the bedroom we share. We fall onto the bed, or I do, he stays behind to unbuckle my shoes, letting each drop to the floor with a soft thud. I have no way to see myself. Edmund stretches out next to me. We stay like that for several minutes, perhaps ten or even fifteen. I can feel my soul being sucked away as he regards me. I cannot bear to be watched at such proximity. Finally he says, I should go paint.

Relieved, I nod and watch his back disappear through the door and out into the hallway. After a moment I cross the room to the bureau and pick up the sunglasses the boy and I bought in Rome. The world turns amber. The glasses still slip down my nose; I still have to push them up again and again. I go down the corridor, passing a window from which I can see Edmund tackling his easel in the rockery. I go into the boy's bedroom. Sheets of newspaper remain on the floor where he left them spread out for polishing his shoes. Our looking away served as our critique; it was never dressed-up despair. No one could ever accuse us of being ill-tempered or peevish. We had everything in Rome, the two of us, everything but money and often food. Our search was affirmative always. Across the room, in the armchair, the boy's green notebook lies crammed between cushions. I cannot remember where we left off. Something about Samina perhaps. I go to the armchair, pick up the notebook and rifle through the pages. The notebook is blank. One or two doodles. Dogs, I think. And faces, some happy, a few sad. Several markings where it appears he may have tested his pen. Nothing more. As it should be. No biographer, no *civilian* could possibly understand what made the seemingly insignificant have such importance to the boy and me on those, our best of days. The boy was quite right to disallow our meaning at the hands of others. They will never know us any better for the pages we leave.

At ten past two the mother leaves to fetch the boy from school. I cannot bear it. In our bedroom, I pull on my buckle shoes and collect Edmund's wristwatch. On down to the kitchen, buckles flapping. Edmund's brother will return full of stories about new friends and experiments, proper ones involving litmus paper and lemons. He will never remember that together we had a science shop where the most famous men of science came to take their coffee. He will want to show his brother a better way to throw or repeat a new joke learned from a chum. The kitchen is empty. Outside Edmund interviews the gardener about my butterfly net. The gardener has a leisurely way of speaking that drives me insane.

On the top shelf of the pantry I find the tin stuffed with cash. I take out a handful of bills and stuff them in my purse along with Edmund's watch and the boy's green notebook. I put the tin back on the shelf, then, on reflection, go back for one or two more bills. Edmund's paintings will bring in thousands of lire. Collectors will arrive from all across Europe. The three of them and their gardener will have no financial worries; they will turn pearish and content.

At the coat stand by the front door I consider taking a walking stick, an umbrella and, inexplicably, a rake. I decide on nothing. The sunglasses slide down my nose as I am shoving my arms into my coat and I am forced to push them up several times before I discern the exact angle I need to tilt my head in order for the glasses to stay put. Then I push the door open; it creaks mightily like the door of a great castle. There it is, that outside world they speak of. The day is looking up again. I take the two front steps as one and begin walking rapidly down the long path that leads to town. I will have plenty of time to skirt the school before the mother brings the boy home. I wager she has taken the boy to a special café for cannoli; he will chatter to her about his new school, the way he once chattered to me about a thousand things. She should not let him have coffee, not without regretting it she shouldn't. Twenty paces down the drive I stop and race back to the house. Bursting through the front door, I pull coats and scarves off their hooks throwing them aside until I find what I am looking for. Oh yes, Mama's hat. I rip off the rose decorating its brim and plant the hat firmly on my head. Then I go out once more, slamming the door behind me. I like the sound so much, I open the door and slam it shut several times. Then I retrace my steps down the long path. I head north toward Rome. That is, in the direction I take for north.

A Note on the Author

Heather McGowan is the author of the novel *Schooling,* which was listed as Best Book of the Year 2001 by *Newsweek,* the *Detroit Free Press,* and the *Hartford Courant.* She lives in Brooklyn.